Sita Brahmachari

KT-215-845

Kite Spirit

C158037717

First published 2013 by Macmillan Children's Books
an imprint of Pan Macmillan
The Smithson, 6 Briset Street, London EC1M 5NR
EU representative: Macmillan Publishers Ireland Limited,
Mallard Lodge, Lansdowne Village, Dublin 4
Associated companies throughout the world
www.panmacmillan.com

ISBN 978-0-330-51792-8

7 9 8 6

A CIP catalogue record for this book is available from
the British Library.

Typeset by Nigel Hazle
Printed and bound by CPI Group (UK) Ltd, Croydon CR0 4YY

Nominated for the UKLA Book Award 2014

To the landscape of the Lake District, where
I lived for a while as a child – long enough for
the mountains, lakes, slate and stone to have
seeped into me . . . and to my Cumbrian family,
past and present, whose lives on fell and farm
are part of the inspiration of this book.

Part One
Falling

Prologue

The Falling Day

Dawn's never late. I check the time again: 8.51. I think I know what's happened now. She must have turned up early, all stressed out, and I had the radio cranked up so loud I didn't hear her knocking. I bet she's already gone and she'll be livid with me later for cutting it so fine. I knock for one last time but it's quiet in her flat. I expect she's been sitting in the exam hall since school opened. That'll be why she's not answering my text either.

I take the remaining communal stairs in twos, practically falling down them as Jess, Dawn's cat, wraps herself around my ankles.

'Go home, Jess! Dawn will be back soon,' I call to her as I sprint down the road, only to find myself stuck behind a pile-up of students. The zebra-crossing lady holds back the traffic for an ambulance followed by a police car, lights flashing, sirens blaring. I wince as the sound grates on me. *What* is the matter with me this morning? I pull myself up straight and take a deep breath. As soon as the crossing's clear I break into a run again, weaving in and out of the stream of students and through the school gates. Once inside I veer off to the right and straight into the hall. The place is eerily quiet considering it's so full. I scan the rows and rows of desks for Dawn but I can't see her anywhere.

'Kite Solomon. One minute later and I would have closed the doors on you,' Miss Choulty whispers.

'What about Dawn?' I ask, checking my phone again to see if she's texted me back yet.

Miss Choulty grabs the phone out of my hands and guides me along the line of little tables.

'The embarrassment of it! Two of my tutor group turning up late . . . and Dawn of all people!' Miss Choulty sighs. We pass an empty desk. 'And as for you, I could have you disqualified for bringing a phone into the exam hall,' she adds, shaking her head. 'Come on, Kite! Sort yourself out. You look half asleep!' Then she seems to read something in my expression and her face softens. 'Never mind about Dawn now – I'm sure there's a perfectly logical explanation. I'll try to find out what's happened; and if I hear anything I'll let you know.' She smiles as she takes hold of my shoulders and physically lowers me into my seat. 'Take a few deep breaths, get a hold of your nerves and you'll do just fine.'

Miss Choulty is my geography teacher and she's

also been our tutor since Year 7. There's not much she won't talk to us about . . . I mean she's even told us that she doesn't think that she can have children of her own. 'Still,' she said after that revelation, 'I'll just put everything I've got into making sure you all grow like sunflowers!' There's something so honest and caring about her that melts even the toughest kids in our school, and she never gives up on anyone. I wasn't even interested in geography before I met her, but she's one of those teachers who makes her subject come alive. She says geography should be renamed 'reading the landscape,' and she presents every lesson as if we're explorers setting out to discover the mysteries of the earth.

Everyone's settled now – everyone, that is, except for Dawn. The place where she should be sitting is three rows forward and one desk to my right. A shrill buzzer sounds, making me jump.

'You may begin,' announces Miss Choulty.

I just stare at Dawn's empty seat, watching pages being turned and notes taken. 'A *perfectly logical explanation*' – Miss Choulty's reassuring words keep running through my head. Maybe there's been some out-of-the-blue family news. But then Dawn hardly ever sees her extended family. Maybe she's ill or something, though it's strange that she didn't say so on Facebook last night. Unless . . . she's just got herself all wound up about the exams. Miss Choulty keeps staring at me. She shakes her pen in the air and starts to mime-write. I pick up my biro. She smiles encouragingly as I print my name: 'Kite Solomon' – and oddly, it feels as if it belongs to someone else. Get a grip, I tell myself as I turn the page and start to scan the paper. The lines of text swim in front of me. I can't make sense of how the words connect together or what they mean. It feels like when I first learned to read. I could say the words out loud, but by the end of the page I would have to get Dawn to explain what it all meant. Dawn's always been miles cleverer than me. If she was here right now she'd already be head down, making notes in the margins and preparing herself to write probably the best GCSE paper ever. I look up at the empty seat. She must be feeling really ill not to turn up. Miss Choulty catches my eye again and frowns. I try to do what she said and hold my nerve. I skim through the whole exam paper from beginning to end before I make an attempt to answer anything.

Glaciation (*of course* this is one of the topics I haven't revised)

1. What is another name for basket of eggs scenery?

I search my brain for everything we've learned, but my mind's meandering all over the place and I can't seem to block out the noises from the street outside. There are always sirens on the main road, but the piercing high-pitched noise blaring out right now seers into me, jangling nerves deep in my jaw, making my teeth ache down to the roots.

'*There's probably a perfectly logical explanation,*' I repeat over and over in my mind.

Just get on with it Kite, I tell myself as I read the next question.

2. Calculate the following coordinates.

The tiny squares of the graph paper mutate into a smudged wave as I try to follow the path along and up, charting where the points should meet. I look at my watch. I can't believe I've been sitting here for over twenty minutes just staring at the questions. Miss Choulty peers at me from beneath her clear-framed glasses as if to say, 'Kite Solomon, what do you think you're doing?' Her voice in my head merges with the sound of the siren, getting louder and . . . closer. I raise my hand. Miss Choulty looks annoyed, but comes over anyway.

'Sorry, miss, I just wondered if you've heard yet why Dawn's not here?'

She looks down at my blank exam paper, scowls and shakes her head.

'I told you I'll let you know if I hear from her,' she whispers. 'Now try to focus. This is important, Kite.'

I wonder if it could be something to do with Dawn's orchestra. All I can hear is the melody of the same phrases she's been practising for months now. Considering I don't even listen to classical music, I probably know more about it than most people just from hearing Dawn on her oboe. When she first started it used to drive me crazy – that high-pitched squeak when she was blowing out her reeds went right through me. But I like the sound now, because I know she's just clearing the airways for what comes next, and that is always beautiful.

A tall woman teacher I've never seen before – probably supply – walks into the back of the hall along the rows of tables and whispers something in Miss Choulty's ear. I can tell by the way Miss Choulty's mouth clamps tight shut that she's trying to hold herself together. She's got one of those faces where you can read every emotion. The blood drains from her cheeks as the woman places a note in front of her. She reads it several times and looks up at me, a deep frown furrowing her forehead. She opens her mouth and seems to gulp the air.

The sirens are quiet now. My gut twists, my stomach tenses. I can't sit here for a moment longer. I push my chair back. I hear it squeak on the wooden floor. I see Miss Choulty raise her hand towards me. I run as fast as I can out of the exam hall, heads turning as I pass like dominoes toppling, the weight of each one felling the next. I feel as if I have stepped out of myself and I'm watching as I run along the corridor across the school bridge. Miss Choulty's calling my name.

I turn to face her and shout at the top of my voice, 'Where's Dawn?'

Miss Choulty runs towards me, reaching out her hands as if she thinks that I might fall. My question echoes back at me along the corridor as she guides me towards Mr Scott's office. Through his half-open door I see a police officer; she has her hand on Mr Scott's shoulder as he sits hunched over his desk. I think how odd it looks for our giant, broad-shouldered head teacher to be comforted by a tiny woman police officer who looks younger than some of the girls in our Sixth Form.

'One moment.' Miss Choulty squeezes my arm and shuts me out of the room. Miss Hopkins on reception, who's usually so cheery and chatty, looks up at me and then quickly away, as if she doesn't dare meet my eye. On her desk is a yellow Post-it note with 'Dawn Jenkins, 22 Fairview Heights' and Dawn's telephone number written on it. Miss Hopkins sees me looking and quickly slips the note in a drawer under her desk.

'A *perfectly logical explanation* . . .' I hear Miss Choulty saying.

'Why have they closed the door on me?' I whisper. I don't even recognize my own voice. Miss Hopkins's eyes are trained on her desk, she doesn't look up at me even for a second, but she has her hand over her mouth as if she's trying to hold something in.

I feel like I did the day I jumped off a rope swing at too high an angle, and I knew that it was only a count of seconds before I'd hear the break of bone against hard earth. Right now I can hear Dawn crying out to me just as she did in those . . . one . . . two . . . three . . . flying seconds.

I'm spiralling down.

Miss Hopkins is offering me tiny sips of water. My legs are splayed out on the floor and one of my black school pumps has fallen off. I should have worn tights today because an icy cold is creeping into me. Miss Hopkins is trying to lift me off the floor. I'm like Dawn's Raggedy Ann doll that's lost her stuffing, as if the insides have been shaken out of me and all my muscles and bones have melted to nothing.

I *know*. Don't ask me how, but at this moment I know that Dawn is gone.

The door opens and Mr Scott is staring down at me. I'm being placed on the comfy sofa. Dawn's been here loads of times with her migraines and her stomach cramps, but I've never sat here before. I sink into the cushions, wishing that I could disappear, but Mr Scott has pulled up a chair and is leaning in close. Miss Choulty perches on the arm of the sofa and holds my hand. Everything inside me says, 'Run! Kite! Run away now before they can tell you anything.' I try to move my legs but they're useless.

'She's always early so she comes up to knock for

me, but not today, so I called for her. I knocked and knocked but there was no answer.' I hear myself talking . . . burbling on and on.

Mr Scott nods and pats my shoulder awkwardly. 'Have you called Kite's parents?' he asks Miss Hopkins.

'On their way,' she replies, finally meeting my eye. She's been crying.

The young police officer, her hair pulled neatly into a tight bun, is speaking quietly into a recording device. She has a tiny oval-shaped birthmark on her neck, just below her ear.

'Dawn has a birthmark,' I say, 'in the shape of a crescent moon. It's funny because that's the same shape she has to make to scrape a perfect reed for her oboe. She spends hours and hours on them, sealing the reed, tying the end so tight to make sure all her breath goes down into the instrument. If a single wisp of air escapes it's terrible because then she can't get the oboe to speak . . . see that's what they call it if you blow and blow and no sound comes. She's shown me how it works loads of times. There's a whole orchestra and you're waiting to come in at exactly the right second but really smooth, no squeaks or splutters.' I hold my fingers to my mouth just as Dawn does whenever she speaks about playing.

I feel Miss Choulty's collarbone stick into me as she wraps her arm around my shoulder.

'You should see how she makes those reeds, Miss

Choulty, the look of concentration on her face. I bought her a little box for her birthday. It holds three, but she's only kept one; she calls it her "golden" reed. When she holds it up to the light you can see inside its little bamboo body: it's got a spine and a heart and everything; that's what they call all the parts – weird, isn't it? – as if it's human!'

I hear my own heart thudding hard against my chest and my voice splinter. I watch the police officer's mouth moving. She's saying my name. 'Yes! Kite – as in what you fly on a windy day.' She's talking to someone at the other end of the phone. Her purple birthmark stretches as the sinews of her neck tense.

'Kite is Dawn's best friend,' Mr Scott explains in his crisp Glaswegian accent. He always chooses his words carefully, he has a way of making opinions sound like facts, but in this case it's true: whatever's happened to Dawn, I *am* her best friend.

The police officer nods sympathetically and walks out of the office and into the corridor.

'Kite Solomon,' I hear her say. 'No! We can't interview her yet. We'll have to wait a few hours – she's still in shock.'

Interview

'Can you tell me when you last spoke to her?

Kite focused on the police officer's birthmark.

'Take your time,' she soothed, patting Kite on the arm and switching on her recorder.

'We Facebooked each other last night. It didn't seem like anything, just chat about the exams and what we'd been doing at the weekend. The only "out of the ordinary" thing, now I think of it, is that she didn't play her oboe.'

'Can you talk me through what happened this morning?' the police officer asked gently.

'I woke up at about seven thirty in a bit of a panic about the exam. Ruby and Seth were already out.'

'Ruby and Seth?'

'My mum and dad. I call them by their first names,' Kite explained as she read the police officer's name badge. 'PC Alison Forster.'

'OK. So you were on your own . . .'

'Yes. I got myself breakfast and switched on the

radio. It was Adele's 'Set Fire to the Rain'. I love that song, Dawn does too, so I cranked it up really loud thinking she might hear it through the ceiling. We do that sometimes, especially if no one's around! I was singing along at the top of my voice and then I played a bit of dance music on my iPod and got really into it and the next thing I knew it was eight thirty. I always think I've got ages and then I'm late. Anyway, I thought something was up because if it wasn't for Dawn I would never be on time for school; she's normally around just before eight thirty. I unplugged my iPod – I thought maybe she'd been knocking and I had the music up so loud I didn't hear. So I grabbed my bag, locked up and ran down the steps between our floor and Dawn's flat. Hazel, Dawn's mum, she's grown sweet peas all along her balcony and I remember thinking it smelt like perfume.' Kite took a deep breath.

'You're doing really well, Kite, carry on.'

'Well, I knocked a few times and called her name. Then Jess, Dawn's cat, came springing out of the flap and got under my feet. I picked her up and she miaowed and miaowed. Her coming out made me think that Dawn must have left because Jess never leaves Dawn's side if she's in the flat. So when I texted her and there was no reply, I thought she must have got fed up waiting for me and gone on ahead. She would have been stressed about the exam so I

14

thought I'd better head in to school. Anyway, I waited by the railings near the zebra crossing and I kept remembering how Jess wouldn't stop wrapping herself around my ankles as if she didn't want me to leave . . . and that's when I got this sick feeling in my belly that something wasn't right.'

'Why was that? Do you think there might have been any warning signs?'

Kite shook her head in answer, but the question kept echoing through her mind. If anyone should have known, surely it was her.

Facebook Memorial

Every night before she laid her head on her pillow, as she did now, Kite took herself back to the day of her exam. She dredged through every detail to see if she had missed something, anything that might have been a 'warning sign'. Sometimes she imagined the story that she'd told the police officer veering off in another direction.

'Take your time.'

Kite stared at the birthmark on the police officer's neck.

I texted her and she texted me back: "I need help". I hurled myself down the steps and kicked at the door to her flat. It took three hard shoves and then the latch gave and I let myself in. Jess miaowed from Dawn's bedroom and I ran through to her. Dawn was just lying there looking pale and ill; there was sick everywhere – the room stank of it.

'What's the matter?' I asked her as I propped her head up.

'I've taken some sleeping pills, a lot of pills,' she told me.

That's when I called the police, and the ambulance came.

The worst thing was that nobody could answer the question that was haunting her day and night. 'What if Dawn *wanted* me to find her?' Kite stood up and walked over to her desk and clicked on the message she wished she could delete from both her Facebook page and her memory forever. Like a moth to a flame, she had read it a thousand tortured times, turning the questions over, searching for a warning sign hidden among those final lines.

Then she scrolled down to read the endless 'Rest in Peace' messages, commemorative photos and shared memories people had posted on the memorial page she'd created. The contributions just kept flooding in.

Part of her regretted setting up the page. Why had she felt the need to do it in the first place? It had taken her ages to find the right words and photos. It had been something to do, she supposed. But she had not been ready for the response. None of these people had really known Dawn at all and yet here they were, claiming that they'd been great friends. It made Kite sick, like watching vultures in a feeding frenzy. At least the messages from Dawn's old orchestra friends felt genuine.

'She played like an angel. I'll miss her. XX Esme'

Kite vaguely remembered this girl from a concert

she'd been to. She was the one who had sat next to Dawn in orchestra and also played the oboe.

Kite could hardly stand to look as new messages of sorrow appeared before her. Seth was right. She should shut herself off from all of this, at least for a while. There was enough going on in her head without it. That's what she *should* do, but once again she found herself reading the last words that had passed between her and Dawn. Words that she now knew off by heart.

Dawn: Where've you been all weekend?

Kite: On my trapeze! Done no revising though! You?

Dawn: A bit!

Kite: Worked all weekend then!?

Dawn: You know me so well!

Kite: Stop worrying! You'll fly like you always do.

Dawn: You're the flyer!

Kite: Working on it!

Dawn: You'll fly like a bird on that cloud swing one day.

Kite: If I'm ever strong enough!

Dawn: You will be. I don't know anyone stronger than you.

Kite: That's cos you hardly know anyone!

Dawn: Funny!

Kite: Gotta go. Ruby's on my case about getting an

early night! See you tomorrow. Don't stay up all night. You can't get higher than an A*.

Dawn: You're an A* friend.

Kite: Don't get all emo on me! You too, 'Sister!'

Dawn's messages never failed to make her smile. That's how it was when you'd known someone all your life and you would always be best friends, no matter what. There was none of the 'If I say this, will it be taken this way or that?' that Kite worried about with other people. The strange thing was that this last exchange had made her smile even more than usual. She imagined it was because when it came down to it, no matter how different they became, they would still be there to wish each other well for the big moments in life. It had always been like this between them, ever since the day in nursery when Dawn had asked Kite, with her four-year-old's lisp, if she would be her 'thithter'.

Now every word of Dawn's last message seemed weighted with a double meaning . . . Why hadn't Kite seen it before? She winced at her jokey attempts to get Dawn to lighten up. If only Ruby hadn't interrupted them when she had . . . if they'd carried on chatting and she'd taken more time to find out what was really going on in Dawn's head, maybe something might have been said that would have changed everything. Kite placed her hands on the keyboard and bashed out the words 'WHY? WHY? WHY?'. The bizarre thing was that she could sense Dawn sitting at her computer downstairs reading her message. Her hands paused over the keyboard. She half expected a reply to come flying back at her like a boomerang, but her urgent question was greeted only with silence.

Kite could not bring herself to name what Dawn had done. In her head, she had come to call it simply the 'S' word. She typed an 'S' on her page and a 'u'. Then deleted the 'u'. She could not think it, or say it, or type it, but what was the alternative? She could not even accept that her friend had 'died', as Jamila, who had known Dawn a bit from music lessons, had written in her kind message.

'I'm so sorry, Kite. I know how close you two were. No one can believe that she's died.'

In Kite's view, people 'died' because they got old or sick, or were caught up in a terrible accident they had no control over. She didn't care that the way you were supposed to describe it now was 'Death by S...' Apparently, the phrase 'Committing S...' was a hangover from the days it was thought of as a crime. But that's exactly how it felt to Kite: a crime. Dying was something that happened to a person, but what Dawn had done, she had done to herself.

What was the other phrase people used? Oh yes, 'passed away'. Kite hated this one more than anything. It was intended to be soothing, as if the person had quietly drifted off to sleep and never woken up. Of course Dawn had fallen into a deep sleep, and quietly too, so that no one else in the world knew that she was drifting away. Not her mum or her dad or even her so-called best friend who had been sleeping in the room above her. Deciding to end your life – what was soothing about that? Kite tried not to think of Dawn's neat little bedroom where they had spent so much time together when they were little, playing dolls, Lego and board games. In the past few years they had listened to music cranked up so loud that it seemed to obliterate the whole world; in that bedroom they had tried on make-up and clothes and plucked their eyebrows disastrously; they had danced and teased each other about their latest crush. That room had felt so full of joy – making Dawn laugh was the one thing Kite had always been able to do.

No, Dawn had not simply 'died' or 'passed away'. There was nothing peaceful about what she'd done. Kite stared at the letter 'S' on her computer screen. They had been in Year 1 when Dawn had taught Kite how to write the perfect 'S'.

sssssssssssssssssssssssssssssssssssssssssssssssssssssssssssssssss
ssssssssssssssssssssssssssssssss

S is for silence, S is for sleep and S is for . . . the unspeakable thing that Dawn had done not only to herself but to everyone around her.

What little sleep Kite could grab these days was

broken by memories of Dawn, and on waking Dawn's presence was so bright and clear that she could almost reach out and touch her. Sometimes, as it was today, Dawn's lemony soap smell lingered through the morning. Kite wondered if she would ever sleep well again, knowing what her friend had done to herself in her bedroom below. She would have liked to scream, to retch, to wash away every memory of Dawn.

She'd overheard Seth and Ruby talking about how strange it was that she hadn't once cried. But to Kite, tears seemed too easy a way to release the turmoil inside her.

Annalisa Pain

At weekends Kite had been one of those people who sprang to life, threw open her curtains and felt a little bubble of excitement rising in her stomach as she considered the multitude of possibilities for the day ahead.

Now Kite slowly pulled aside her curtains on to a pitifully grey day. She looked up at the dull sky and felt as if the roof of her world had been lowered.

'It's that Annalisa Pain again, from Circus Space!' Ruby knocked, gently opened the door and held the phone out.

'Tell her I'm not coming.'

Ruby placed her head on one side and paused to look at her daughter. Kite gazed back blankly. She had the oddest feeling of looking at her mother critically, as a stranger might have seen her. She noticed that Ruby had new nail extensions with little sequins sparkling in half-moons at the tips. Ruby glided towards the bed and sat down beside Kite. She was a graceful woman with velvety dark, unlined skin, it was impossible to tell what age she was, partly because she was so fit from all her dancing and choreography. She wore shocking pinks and mustards, or lime greens with purples, and always a thick dramatic Cleopatra line skilfully drawn along her eyelids. Sometimes, as she had today, she twisted silver and golden threads into her long braids and added 'a bit of shimmer' to her eyes. Looking again at her sequinned nails, Kite winced inside at Ruby's refusal to blend in. Until now Kite had always been proud that her mum didn't, sheep-like, conform to a bland standard.

It was way back in nursery when Dawn had first made her realize that Ruby and Seth were a bit 'different'.

'Why don't you call them Mum and Dad?' Dawn asked.

'Because they're Seth and Ruby.' Kite shrugged.

'And why did they call you Kite?'

'They said I chose it myself. They went for a walk and I was being carried in my baby sling and I kicked my legs cos I saw a kite flying.'

'So what did they call you before?'

'Nothing – Ruby and Seth think babies should choose their own names!'

'That's silly! Babies can't talk!' Dawn giggled.

'I suppose!'

Kite still remembered the odd shifting feeling

inside her that day when Dawn had first come for tea. Ruby and Seth had told her the story of her naming so many times that she could almost picture her baby self reaching out and grasping her name from a sky full of floating possibilities.

'What's a hippy?' Dawn asked.

'I don't know.

'Ruby! What's a hippy?' Kite asked at tea later.

'Why?'

'That's what my mum and dad said you are,' Dawn answered.

'That may be so!' Ruby laughed.

There was something about hearing four-year-old Dawn's thoughts that made Kite smile, until she remembered. Ruby smoothed Kite's cheek as if she had glimpsed in her fleeting expression a tiny ray of hope. Kite pushed Ruby's sparkling hands away. Today she wished that the world could be as colourless and numb as she felt.

'Annalisa thinks the training might do you good,' Ruby coaxed. 'What shall I tell her?'

'I've told you I'm *not* going.' Kite burrowed her head under the pillow. Why couldn't they understand that she just wanted to be left alone?

'OK, darlin', you take your time,' Ruby soothed, her soft, lilting Caribbean accent always at its strongest when she was concerned about someone. Ruby promised Annalisa that she would call her later, hung up and eased the pillow away from Kite's face.

'Do you want to talk?' she asked, gently tucking a coil of Kite's hair behind her ear. Kite pulled away and turned her head to face the mattress.

'Does it look like I want to talk?'

'When you're ready, my love, we're here.' Ruby sighed deeply as she stood up, walked quietly out of the room and closed the door behind her.

Kite had always been able to tell Ruby and Seth anything that sprang into her mind. No subject was off-limits, but now she felt as if they were living in separate universes and there was no way that she could talk to them because the Kite she was now *felt* so far from the Kite she had been only a few days before. She knew it was unfair to take it out on her mum, but she was sick of being told what would be good for her. She had overheard people saying things like, 'If she would only get a bit of exercise, it might take her out of herself.' Where did they think she would go if she wasn't *in* herself? It was as if everyone thought that, given enough time, she would forget Dawn, move on and get back to 'normal'. Why couldn't they understand that what Dawn had done had changed everything forever; even the things that she had treasured about their past together were sullied now.

Why would she want to go down to Circus Space

and turn herself upside down on the trapeze, of all things? Her ambition to fly on the cloud swing, the highest of all trapezes, seemed so ridiculous now. She wished that she had never met Annalisa and got caught up with the whole scene at Circus Space. Maybe then she'd have had time to notice what was going on with Dawn.

'I'll only be an hour or so! I'm helping out a friend with a bit of choreography,' Ruby called as she disappeared into one of the studios.

That 'hour or so' turned into a yawning three hours. Sick of waiting, Kite wandered into a vast brick warehouse to find a woman arcing through the air like a great bird of prey. At the sight of her, something within Kite clicked into place, as if she'd discovered what she was meant to do, meant to be. Watching the woman fly made Kite's heart leap out of her body and gave her a surging feeling of hope that anything was possible.

Then there was the day she'd gone over to Dawn's to break the news about training with Annalisa. She remembered the nagging feeling in her gut that the new friends she was making at Circus Space would take her away from Dawn. 'Don't worry! You and me are *always* going to be best friends,' Dawn had reassured her. Actually it had felt, at that moment, more like a promise. Kite had been so relieved that she threw her arms around Dawn and hugged her tight.

Dawn had always been able to read Kite's thoughts. She was just that sort of person, noticing things about people, being sensitive to their moods.

'Lighten up!' Dawn joked, as she pulled away from Kite. They did that sometimes, just for the hell of it, changed scripts. 'So? What's she like, this Annalisa?'

Kite sprang up on to Dawn's mattress with such enthusiasm that she nearly bounced Dawn off the end of the bed and tumbled to the floor herself.

Dawn broke her fall. 'Steady.' She giggled.

'She's quite amazing-looking – really tall with this dyed blonde hair, almost white. It's so short it practically looks shaved, and you've never seen arms and legs as long as hers, not even yours!' Kite joked, as Dawn tucked her legs under her. 'After she'd finished this unbelievable routine on the cloud swing she somersaulted her way down a rope and I waited for her at the bottom! I went over to say how good she was but before I could, she just stuck her chin in the air and marched past me. Then I followed her into this cafe area and started talking to her anyway. You should have seen the way she looked at me, peering down from her long neck. Come to think of it, she does look a bit like a swan!'

'She sounds kind of awe-inspiring!'

'She is! She kept trying to fob me off though, but eventually she said she'd give me a trial!'

'That's what I love about you – once you've got an

idea in your head you'll never give up!' Dawn smiled.

'What? And you would?!' Kite retorted, climbing back up on to the bed and peering down at Dawn imperiously. 'What eez your name?' she asked in what was meant to be Annalisa's French accent.

They played this game a lot. Kite had discovered when they were in Year 1 what an amazing knack Dawn had of mimicking people. She said it was because she was an outsider so she had the time to observe them from a distance, unlike Kite, who was more a part of things. Kite was always trying to get Dawn to put herself forward for plays, but she never would. She amazed everyone when she acted a part in drama lessons though. She'd even played Ruby once, slipping into her light Caribbean accent and making Kite roar with laughter with her over-the-top dancer's gesticulations.

'Nice to meet you, Annalisa, I'm Kite!' said Dawn, perfectly capturing Kite's equally proud upright stance and direct gaze.

'You cannot be serious!' laughed Kite throwing back her head in a ridiculously exaggerated Annalisa gesture that sent Dawn off into a giggling fit.

'Sounds like you've found your thing,' Dawn smiled when they'd stopped messing around. 'I knew you would. You're as much of a perfectionist as me in your own way.'

'I suppose I am, once it's something I want to do.

Like you with your oboe. You've got to really love that instrument to bother with all that reed-scraping stuff!' Kite walked over to Dawn's desk. A pile of thread and bamboo shavings littered the surface.

'Maybe.' Dawn shrugged.

Dawn often asked Kite what she thought of the sound of each new reed, and Kite had tried to explain that she could never hear the difference between the ones Dawn rejected and snapped and the ones that 'showed promise'.

'Don't you want to keep the reeds you've really enjoyed playing?' Kite asked.

'Maybe this one from the Brahms concert you came to see me in,' Dawn pondered, picking up a reed that she'd tied with golden thread.

'You should – you were brilliant that night.'

Dawn shrugged, cradling the reed in her cupped hand as if it alone was responsible for her playing well.

Later, through her bedroom wall, she heard Dawn practising the same phrase over and over again. It sounded like she was punishing herself for something.

Tragic Loss of Perfect Dawn

'You talk of her as if she's still here,' Miss Choulty commented.

It was true. Kite could not stow Dawn away neatly into the past like everyone else seemed able to do with their 'She *was* so clever' . . . 'She *had* such potential' . . . 'She *was* an outstanding musician' . . . 'She always *used* to' . . . That would feel like packing her away in a big chest, closing the lid, carrying her up to an old cobwebby loft and switching off the light forever. But the way she saw it, it was Dawn who had abandoned *her*.

When Miss Choulty had called around for a 'chat' Kite had been the only one in. The teacher hadn't waited for an invitation. She'd walked straight in, as Kite stood frozen in the doorway.

'Your mum suggested I call. She told me you're having trouble sleeping,' Miss Choulty said as she patted the sofa for Kite to sit down next to her.

A blast of inexplicable anger towards Ruby flared

31

up inside her. Why couldn't her mum just leave her alone?

'What do you miss about her?' Miss Choulty asked as Kite stared down at her hands.

'I miss her music most of all,' Kite replied eventually. Actually it had often driven Kite mad as Dawn repeated a phrase over and over on her oboe, going over every note until she'd got it exactly right, but then when she played the whole piece through, usually right at the end of the day, you could never hear the joins and her playing transported you somewhere else . . . More often than not it had lulled Kite into a peaceful sleep.

Kite could picture the scene right now of the day in school when they'd all been offered the chance to learn an instrument. She'd chosen the violin and given up in less than a month, but from the first day Dawn had been fascinated by the oboe. She had practised so hard that within a year she was playing pieces that put everyone else to shame. And then she'd been given free lessons and the bursary to buy her oboe, and that had been her life from then on.

'I told that police officer. She didn't play, on the night before . . . not a single note, nothing, and now I think about it, she'd been practising less and less,' Kite explained to Miss Choulty.

Could she have seen it coming? Suddenly it seemed possible to spot signs everywhere, not only the night before what she had come to think of as the Falling Day, the day her whole life had begun to fall apart. And she felt as if she was still falling.

Miss Choulty rubbed Kite's arm to remind her that she was in the room.

'What did she like to play?'

'I don't really know the names of the composers and pieces, except for the concert I went to. Brahms. I can't remember which symphony. I'll get the programme if you want?'

Miss Choulty nodded, and Kite went through to her bedroom and rummaged in her drawer.

'Brahms's Symphony No. 1,' Miss Choulty read out as she traced her fingers down the list to find . . . 'First Oboe – Dawn Jenkins.' She bit her bottom lip. 'Such a waste,' she whispered. A tiny silver St Christopher resting in the bony enclave of her collarbone rose with her uneven breath. Kite wondered how she had never noticed it before. St Christopher was Grandma Grace's favourite saint too.

'Darlin', don't you just love the image of this great giant muscle man carrying the child to safety over the rough surging river. And his back does ache, and his arms does ache because he don't even know yet he is carrying the creator of the world on his shoulder!'

It was good to hear her grandma's lilting voice in her ear, comforting.

'Now, child, even if you say you don't believe, one

day I will give you my St Christopher. He protects the children all over the wide world, you know.'

'Sorry, Kite!' Miss Choulty sniffed as she blew her nose and wiped away her tears.

'Sometimes when she plays her oboe at night it helps me get to sleep,' Kite whispered. Miss Choulty leaned forward, as if hopeful that Kite would continue. But that was all she had to say. After a period of silence, Kite didn't even look up as Miss Choulty said her goodbyes and left.

How could she describe to anyone how much she missed Dawn, that her silence was like a clamouring emptiness filled only with Kite's unanswered questions? '*What if* I could have done something to help her? *What if* I'd knocked harder? *What if* I'd kicked down her door and gone inside? *What if* the ambulance had been called earlier? *What if* I'd seen her the night before and talked instead of just Facebooking? *What if* I'd never got involved at Circus Space? *What if* I'd been more sensitive? *What if* I'd asked more questions? Been a better listener? *What if . . . ? What if . . . ? What if . . . ?*'

And then the *Whys* would start. '*Why* couldn't she talk to me and tell me what was going on in her head?' Kite asked herself over and over. But this was a tortured phrase of music and Kite would never be able to fix the joins in it now, no matter how hard she tried.

Sleepless Night

It should have been a relief to be in her own room that night, away from all the questions and phone calls and visits. She knew that her friends from her running club were only being kind by calling around, but she couldn't bring herself to go back to the things she'd done before. It would feel like saying that everything was back to normal. She didn't even know where they'd taken Dawn's body. Nobody seemed to want to answer her questions, but she had seen enough films to imagine that Dawn was probably lying in some ice-cold mortuary. Even the words filled her with horror. 'Mortuary . . . autopsy,' – they sounded like a kind of dissection. Why did it all have to take so long? Why couldn't they just let Dawn be?

Jacey and Laura had called around *again* this morning and she'd told them straight that she wouldn't run until after the funeral. It wasn't exactly true. Only yesterday she'd found herself putting on her trainers and attempting to jog around the park –

but instead of the familiar feeling of freedom as she pounded the pathway, her legs felt heavy and her chest tightened, as if someone was squeezing her lungs in a vice. She had only been going for ten minutes before her legs began to shake. Kite doubted that she would ever feel the urge to run again.

Whenever Ruby or Seth persuaded her to venture out of the flat she drew sympathetic nods and found herself locked into strained conversations in which people told her how sorry they were, and she'd automatically say 'thank you', as if it meant anything to her that people she hardly knew, and who didn't really know Dawn, were sorry. She'd decided that it was better to be on her own. The problem was, alone in her room she bombarded herself with more questions than anyone else had thought to ask her.

Kite stood up and walked over to her long mirror. Her skin, normally a rich brown colour, had taken on a sallow yellowish tinge. Her huge moss-green eyes were sunken into her face. She stretched her arms towards the ceiling and felt the same strangled stiffness as when she'd tried to run. She would have liked to raise her head to the sky and howl, but no sound came. She dropped her shoulders and hung her head so that her coils of thick black, copper-lit hair brushed over her feet. The rush of blood to her brain made her dizzy and the backs of her legs ached. Until now she had always felt that her body could carry her anywhere she wanted to go, but since the Falling Day she had a growing sensation of standing outside herself, watching events, with no power to change anything.

Instead of sleeping she found herself wandering around her room doing and thinking the most random things. She sat at her computer and googled Brahms to find out what sort of a man he was. As if knowing about Dawn's favourite composer would provide her with the answers she needed.

'The music of Brahms shows a passionate nature turned in on itself.'

She read the sentence over and over again. Maybe this is how Dawn had felt too, distant from the world and everyone in it.

Kite stared at herself in the mirror again. 'Dawn Jenkins is Kite Solomon's best friend,' she said out loud. And who was Kite Solomon without Dawn? Maybe because she had known Dawn for longer than anyone except for her parents, she had never realized how far her sense of who she was, was bound up with Dawn.

Kite could picture Dawn on her sixteenth birthday, only three weeks ago. Her fine auburn hair was pulled back into a ponytail, her soft hazel eyes heavily lined with black. She'd worn skinny jeans and a tight long-sleeved T-shirt with an abstract line drawing in the centre, and the locket that Kite had bought for her when they'd left primary school. It contained a photo of eleven-year-old Kite in one side and eleven-year-old Dawn in the other. She was willowy slim and tall, with legs that seemed to go on forever, but Dawn could never see how beautiful she was, always going on instead about how lucky Kite was not to have grown too much, what a pain it was to have curves and boobs and have to wear a bra.

Every time they looked in the mirror Dawn would compliment Kite on her eclectic style, admiring her latest quirky buy from Camden market and her DMs, her coils of hair, her smooth brown skin, her slightly upward-turning nose, the beauty spot on her right cheekbone, and what Dawn called her perfect 'Angelina Jolie' mouth.

'Yes, well. You make me sound perfect. This!' Kite laughed, pointing to her beauty spot, 'is actually more of a mole, and what about the spots I'm hiding under my hair?' She lifted up her tangle of curls to reveal a fine rash of spots she got every month around the time of her period. 'And how come you completely forget to mention my scar-brow!'

Kite's scar was about a centimetre long and it cut through her right eyebrow like an arrow: the hair would never grow there. She'd got it on the day she'd jumped off the rope swing and crashed headfirst into the ground, Dawn crying out in horror. The wound had gushed blood with a frightening force, but once it was all cleaned up and stitched it wasn't really that big a deal. Because of her wild hair most people didn't notice the scar, or perhaps they were too polite to mention it. It didn't really bother Kite, but according to Dawn she had a habit whenever she was nervous of pulling on her hair to cover it up.

Now she thought of it, Dawn's sixteenth birthday had been the last time she'd been in Dawn's room. As she'd watched Dawn applying her make-up Kite had noticed how cracked and dry Dawn's skin had become; the worst that she'd seen it in a long time.

'I can completely get rid of that scar, if you want me to,' she told Kite as she finished making up her own face. 'Can you see my birthmark?' She turned to the side. Kite shook her head. Dawn had taken to masking the mark with foundation, powder and concealer.

'OK! I've often wondered what I'd look like without it!' Kite agreed, staring at her scar in the little hand mirror.

Dawn went to work on her with her toolkit collection of make-up, powdering, buffing and drawing in the gap in her eyebrow with a pencil and eyeshadow.

'Perfect! You look like a model,' Dawn smiled when she was done.

Kite stared at herself in the mirror. Her scar was completely gone, but she felt like a painted doll someone had given her as a child that had freaked her out and given her nightmares.

'Maybe, but I don't even recognize myself!' she laughed and went over to the corner sink to wash the make-up off while Dawn buffed another layer of powder over her birthmark.

'Why do you always have to wear so much make-up? You don't need it,' Kite asked, slumping down on Dawn's bed as she dried her face.

Dawn shrugged and walked over to the sink, smoothed her tongue over her teeth, and flossed carefully. Afterwards she took her lemon-scented soap and began her ritual hand washing.

'I do actually – my skin looks dull without it,' Dawn finally answered.

Dawn's parents had given the newspapers her last school photo in which she'd made herself up perfectly, just as she had on her birthday. The headline in the newspaper read: 'Tragic Loss of Perfect Dawn'. When she'd seen it Kite had wished that Hazel and Jimmy had provided a more natural photo to show the world how gentle and young Dawn really was. Now, thinking back to her birthday, Kite wondered . . . If Dawn had not been wearing her make-up mask, would she have confided in her how she'd been feeling? She racked her mind for what else they had talked about on that day.

'Has he asked you out yet?' Kite asked.

'Who?'

'Mr Saxy! The clarinet player I saw making eyes at you at the concert – the one you said "plays the sax like a dream too".'

'Funny!' Dawn blushed bright red from the neck up and changed the subject. 'How's it going with you and Mali then?'

Mali was a boy Kite had met at Circus Space. He juggled mostly and was training on the giant globe hoop. She loved to watch him turning upside down. He reminded her of that da Vinci drawing of the man with all his muscles showing, turning on an axel. Kite had let slip to Dawn that they'd joked around a bit when they'd been training, but when they'd kissed she'd felt nothing. It had been Kite's fourth kiss, and the best yet, but still not that special.

'Well, at least you're not sixteen and never been kissed!' Dawn joked.

'Never by anyone I really *wanted* to kiss!'

After that Kite had handed over her present: the little reed box with the green velvet lining. Dawn had cried as she'd inspected the soft leather box.

'It was supposed to make you happy!'

'Best present you've ever given me.' Dawn hugged her tightly.

She'd bought it while Dawn spent hours searching for what might turn out to be 'a golden reed'. Kite had thought Dawn mad when she'd told her that her favourite place in the world was Howarth's wind instrument shop, until the day she'd gone there herself.

Kite stepped inside Howarth's smart door, ran her fingers over the smooth wooden counters, and watched the man in the old fashioned hessian apron and double rimmed spectacles taking out a tray of reeds.

'Smell that!' Dawn sighed as she breathed in the rich oboe resin.

Dawn led Kite along a wall of oboes sniffing as they went like a couple of dogs picking up a scent, making each other giggle as usual. Dawn was inspecting a basket full of bamboo. She picked up a stick and felt its weight.

'This bamboo's from a farm in France. It's the one my teacher makes her reeds from!' Dawn explained.

Kite peered down. To her it was nothing more than a stick.

On the way out they passed a wall of portraits of famous wind musicians.

'I bet you'll have your picture up there one day!' Kite commented as they walked out of the shop.

'I doubt it!' Dawn replied.

I doubt it.

No matter how much people told Kite not to rake over things she couldn't help casting back to these moments. Her mind was like an endlessly whirring film reel with scenes cut up in the wrong order, flitting backwards and forward in time, desperately trying to search out what might have been a cry for help. But how could she have known? Everyone her age had insecurities about something.

As she looked back on the scene, knowing what she knew now, she couldn't understand why she hadn't screamed at Dawn to stop worrying about things that didn't matter instead of trying to shrug everything off with a joke.

What else had they talked about? It was all coming back to her now.

'Somewhere down the line most of them are probably related to Brahms or Mozart!' Dawn joked. 'At least Ruby and Seth know about music and art and stuff like that. I never would have got that scholarship for music school without your dad's help. My mum and dad don't know about that stuff.'

'But look how proud they are of you. Photos and certificates on every wall . . .'

Dawn groaned.

'And remind me! Who've they made the first oboe in your posh orchestra?'

She wished now that she had sat and listened to what Dawn was trying to say. Instead she had changed the subject and started complaining about Ruby and Seth.

'It's all very well for you; you don't have to live with them!' Kite laughed. 'Or a name like Kite!'

'Dawn.' Kite spoke her friend's name into the mirror, letting the tip of her tongue rest on the roof of her mouth. It was as if she was saying the name for the first time. And for the first time, she registered the meaning of her friend's name.

Dawn is only the break of day, the beginning, you can't end at the beginning, Kite pleaded. But who was she pleading with? Her head clamped as if someone was tightening the pressure inside her mind. Until the Falling Day she had never once experienced the headaches that had gripped Dawn so suddenly and so often. She scrunched up her eyes and wished as hard as she had ever wished for anything that she could fall asleep and wake up in the nursery playground on the day that she and Dawn first met, peer down through the playground ladders of long ago and start all over again . . . at their beginning.

Climbing Frame

I'm standing at the top of the red ship climbing frame; a girl is underneath on the grass. She's looking down at the ground so I can't see her face, but she's got a long neat plait and she's wearing shiny shoes. They're brand-new navy blue, no scuffs on them at all. I look down at my new trainers, already caked in mud.

'Will you be my thithter?' the girl lisps.

It's cold and I can see her breath forming in the air, like ghost whispers. Her voice is high and sweet and it floats straight up to me. She sort of smiles. I haven't got a sister or a brother so I say, 'OK! Climb up then!'

She takes ages, crawling on her hands and knees over the wooden bars. She's clinging on so tight that her knuckles turn white. I give her my hand and she takes it and stands up. It's funny because she didn't look very tall from down there.

It was difficult to know now as Kite looked back through time whether she was doing what everyone else was, reinventing Dawn, reading into things that had never been there; back then Kite would probably have described those soft hazel eyes as shy, but maybe there had been a sadness lurking there too. Kite squeezed her own eyes tight shut and tried to imagine herself flying on the cloud swing. It was what all her training on the trapeze was for, so that one day she would be strong enough to fly between great oak trees performing at some open air-festival floodlit beneath the stars. But it felt like a childish dream now. Everything was spoilt, even her dreams. For the first time all this seemed nothing more than a fantasy. Now when she thought of it she felt no wings fluttering in her belly, no kite spirit rising.

Her stomach burned with a bitter, angry feeling that she couldn't make sense of. She wished she could find a way of delving inside herself, grabbing hold of it and tearing it out. I only need to understand why she did it, Kite told herself. Maybe then she would be able to cry, to sleep . . . to feel something like her old self again.

The Valley of Death

Ruby had said the funeral would help, give everyone a proper opportunity to say goodbye to Dawn, for Kite to finally cry . . . and after that . . . to sleep.

Kite was standing a few rows back from the simple wooden coffin. Hazel and Jimmy stood alone in the small pew closest to Dawn, Jimmy's arm enveloping Hazel's slumped shoulders. A handful of people Kite had never seen before gathered in the pews surrounding Jimmy and Hazel. Behind her the little chapel was filling up; some friends of Jimmy and Hazel from work were wearing their hospital uniforms. The whole thing felt clinical. There were no flowers. Everyone had been asked to make donations to a charity of their choice instead. Ruby had donated money to ChildLine because she'd volunteered for them in the past. She'd tried to involve Kite in a discussion about why it was so important to see the bereavement counsellor their GP has offered.

'Sometimes, my darlin', it's easier to talk about your

feelings to someone with no connection to you,' she'd explained. Kite had remained silent. There was no way that she could tell a total stranger all the thoughts that were passing through her head right now.

The 'no flowers' request felt sensible but it seemed so cold to leave the coffin bare, as if no one cared. Ruby stood to one side of her and Seth to the other, like bodyguards, Kite thought. There was a heavy silence full of questions and misery. The only person who could answer the insistent cry of 'Why? Why? Why?' that echoed through this silence was lying in that coffin.

Kite glanced around and found Miss Choulty's compassionate smile. To one side of her were three students in school uniform. She recognized them from Dawn's music class. Jamila had swapped her green headscarf for a white one. She too smiled at Kite sadly. To Miss Choulty's other side sat two women, whispering loudly.

'Had high hopes for her . . . So proud with her music grades and everything! I was just talking to her teacher. She reckons she was set for Oxford or Cambridge for certain . . .'

Kite's gut twisted as hot acid seemed to fill the well from which her tears should have drawn. The thought of all these people gathering to bury Dawn felt so wrong, like a nightmare that she'd got herself stuck inside.

In the pew in front of her stood a tall man in a long black coat. He had thick greying hair, and beside him stood a boy with a messy mane of his own. It took Kite a while to place them. Of course! They were from Dawn's orchestra: the conductor and the saxophonist Kite had teased Dawn about. The man had his arm wrapped around the boy in a comforting gesture. Next to them stood a tall girl wearing a short black skirt, ballet pumps and a cream long-sleeved top. As she turned in profile Kite recognized her too – this was Esme from the Brahms concert. Her shiny blonde hair shone like ripe wheat as she now walked to the front of the church with her oboe. It looked somehow swankier than Dawn's. The wood was dark and rich and the silver keys gleamed.

Kite watched her take a deep breath and begin to play with a confidence she had never seen in Dawn. The notes sang out in the echoey church. Kite closed her eyes and listened. She understood exactly why Dawn had been made the principal in her orchestra. There was nothing technically wrong with Esme's playing, no false notes, and the music sounded smooth and sweet. But when Dawn played there was a raw truth that made you stop and listen. Now, hearing Esme, Kite understood that Dawn had spoken everything that was in her heart through her music. It *was* her way of speaking. As she listened she was amazed to see that the boy who stood in front of her was racked with sobs.

The fact that all these people had cared so much for Dawn made what she had done even more difficult to fathom. There was nothing that Hazel and Jimmy would not have done to help her 'get on in the world'. Kite had been touched by the way they talked of 'the world', as if it was somewhere they had no place in but somehow, miracle of miracles, they'd had a daughter who *was* worthy. Or could have been. Watching the boy wipe his tears away made Kite feel like opening the lid of the coffin, grabbing hold of Dawn's shoulders and shaking her alive. 'Look how loved you are!' she wanted to scream.

I should have spoken, Kite thought as she watched Esme return to her seat beside the grief-stricken boy.

When Jimmy had called round to ask if she would like to say a few words at Dawn's funeral she'd said that she was afraid she wouldn't be able to.

'Don't you worry,' he'd said. 'I'm not sure I'll be able to speak myself, and Hazel can't take the pressure of it. You were a great friend to Dawn. That's better than words,' he'd told her as he left, and this phrase had come back to haunt her. She stared at Dawn's coffin. How could I have been a great friend if you felt so awful that you took your own life and I didn't even know how bad you were feeling?

Jimmy stood up in his smart suit, the one she'd

seen him wearing only once, a few weeks ago, when they'd passed on the stairs.

'On my way to a job interview. Wish me luck, Kite! If I get it, it'll be the end of shift work for me!' he'd said, unbuttoning his jacket. 'Shows how often I wear this. It only gets an airing at weddings and funerals. Think I might have put on a few pounds since I last wore it,' he'd joked, tapping his round tummy.

As Jimmy stood at the front of the chapel, clasping his speech, she noticed that the suit jacket looked too big for him, as if he had stepped into someone else's clothes. His whole frame seemed to have shrunk.

Ruby reached into her handbag for tissues. Her hands looked small too, without their usual nail extensions and bright polish. Kite glanced up at Ruby's face. She wore no make-up, giving herself over to the fact that the day would be full of tears. Seth reached over and placed his arm around both of them. As Kite watched Jimmy take a deep breath to speak she found herself standing up, pushing past Seth and walking to the front of the chapel to sit next to Hazel. It felt wrong that she should be sitting there alone. Hazel turned to Kite with a look of utter confusion and emptiness. Her hollow cheeks were stained with tears and her nose was streaming, but she didn't seem to notice. As Jimmy began to speak Kite reached for Hazel's hand, but Hazel did not register her touch. The tips of her fingers were ice cold. It was as if something inside her had died too.

'Our daughter . . .' Jimmy paused and coughed as he struggled to speak her name.

'Our daughter, Dawn Melissa Jenkins, was our pride and our joy.' He held up what looked like a long handwritten speech, but the tears fell heavily from his eyes and dripped on to the paper. He stared at the bare coffin and the paper floated to the ground. He stood in silence for a moment while he collected himself and looked out over the mourners at the round stained glass window at the far end of the chapel. Kite followed his eyes to the grim image of Christ's crucifixion on a wooden cross. 'She was our hope and our happiness.' He bent down and picked up the piece of paper. 'I wrote this speech about what she meant to us. I'm sorry, I've got no heart to read it now, but Miss Choulty, Dawn's teacher, has a few words she wants to say.' Jimmy bowed his head and walked back to his seat. As he sat down he nodded at Kite as if to say thank you for sitting with Hazel.

Miss Choulty was wearing a neat navy-blue suit. Her St Christopher glinted around her neck as she opened a little notebook and began to speak. Her familiar voice blurred into a strain of sadness. Kite did not hear the individual words that she spoke except for when she said how full of 'potential' Dawn had been. At this, Hazel let out a cry so strange and deep that Miss Choulty stopped and lost her place in her speech, leaving the whole congregation flailing around in silence. She uttered a few more words and returned to her seat. There were hymns; 'All Things Bright and Beautiful' was the only one Kite recognized. The organ seemed to play a beat behind the congregation as if it was dragging a heavy load uphill. Nobody sang with much enthusiasm. Jimmy, Hazel and Kite remained silent.

After the priest had said a few words about the 'tragic circumstances of this loss for family, school and community' and how Dawn would be 'welcomed into the Kingdom of Heaven like a Lamb of God', and after people had muttered their 'Amens', everyone followed the coffin bearers out to the patch of ground that had been prepared for Dawn. Kite peered down into the deep hole that had been dug where now a murky pool of water was forming. Jimmy followed Kite's gaze into the hole and as he did two great tears rolled down his face and dropped into the filthy mud puddle. Jimmy and Hazel clung together, holding each other up. Hazel's face was still blank, as if her kind, lively spirit had flown out of her. Kite recognized something of how she herself felt mirrored in Hazel's eyes.

'You can't let her go into that hole,' Kite called out suddenly. Seth and Ruby stood on either side of her, holding her close and steady, but as the young priest committed Dawn's body to the earth and talked of 'walking through the valley of death and fearing no evil', his own strength seemed to falter. He nodded at Kite briefly and took a deep breath before continuing.

After the ceremony was over he sought her out.

'That was my first funeral,' he explained.

'Mine too,' Kite whispered back.

'So hard to bury someone this young.' Kite sensed that he was trying to coax her into talking.

'Do you have faith?' he continued.

Kite shrugged. She thought of Miss Choulty's St Christopher and Grandma Grace, who was a fellow devotee. If she could pray for anything right now, she would ask for St Christopher to have appeared to Dawn, like a miracle, lifted her in his arms and carried her out of the depths of her sadness.

'I understand that this is not your church, but if you ever want to talk . . .'

Kite felt a gentle hand on her shoulder and turned away from the priest with a mumbled, 'Thanks.'

'Are you Kite?' she asked.

Kite nodded.

'I'm Esme!' the girl said. 'She talked about you all the time . . .' She waited for a response, but no words came to Kite. 'I wish she hadn't been so shaken by that last concert,' Esme continued. 'It was only temporary, you know, me replacing her on first oboe, just to take the pressure off for a bit. She was always so much better than me.'

Kite felt as if she was listening to Esme through a shroud of fog.

'What do you mean?'

'Didn't she tell you?' Esme looked shocked. 'At the last concert we played she froze during the first solo. We told her it happens to everyone sometimes, you just have to ignore it and carry on, but instead she laid her oboe on her knee and stopped, just stopped. Like she'd given up. My dad, he's the conductor –' she nodded over to the tall man in the black coat – 'he didn't have a choice, I had to take her solos for the rest of the concert. I didn't want to. I kept checking to see if she'd start playing again.' Esme's shoulders were shaking and the tears streamed down her clear rosy cheeks. 'It was torture – she just sat there for the whole concert. What made it even worse was that there were some important people who'd come especially to hear her play.'

Kite could almost feel the heat in her friend's face as she sat exposed and humiliated, willing the concert to end. It had been nearly two years since she'd gone to watch Dawn at her first full-blown recital, when she'd played her favourite Brahms symphony and she'd looked so happy. Kite had seen her in loads of things since then, playing like a professional. How could it all have gone so badly wrong?

'But I only went with her to Howarth's a few weeks ago, to buy more reeds.' Kite grabbed hold of Esme's arms and shook her. 'What do you mean, she froze? When was this? She didn't tell me anything.'

'I'm sorry, I thought . . .' Esme pulled away from Kite's tight grip. 'Dad and I, and even Eddie, phoned her,' Esme explained, looking over at the boy who had been so distressed, 'to tell her we needed her back.' She wouldn't answer our calls, so in the end Dad sent a letter to her parents to meet and talk everything through. But they never replied.'

'I don't understand . . . she was at rehearsal every Saturday.'

Esme shook her head. 'We haven't seen her for nearly two months now.'

'Then Hazel and Jimmy can't have got that letter . . . They didn't know either. She must have felt so alone.'

The boy with the black hair came and stood next to Esme. 'Kite, this is Eddie.'

'I've seen you play.'

The boy nodded, his dark eyes red and swollen.

'I told her you liked her but she wouldn't believe me.'

The boy opened his mouth to speak then hesitated and closed it again.

'Kite was Dawn's closest friend,' Esme explained.

'I wasn't,' whispered Kite. 'I can't have been or she would have told me what was going on in her head.'

'I'm sorry,' whispered Esme, and she and Eddie

seemed to float off into the crowd of mourners.

Kite wished she could cry. It was as if she had become an instrument with only two notes – flat and sharp; she was either dull and empty or filled with bitter acid anger that made her want to lash out at someone or something. Suddenly the sky darkened and the rain began to fall. Umbrellas sprung open and people scurried away to take cover in the eaves of the chapel.

'Come in from the rain, Kite,' Seth called over the din of the downpour as he sprinted towards her with his umbrella. She shook her head at his offer of protection. Instead she stood in the middle of the courtyard and held out her arms. It was a relief to be bombarded by something as simple and clean as rain.

Kite Song

Kite heard the doorbell but pretended to be asleep on the day that Mr Scott called round to discuss the possibility of finishing her exams. Through her bedroom wall she could just about make out the gist of his conversation with her mother. It seemed to be going around and around in circles until Ruby raised her voice.

'Let the child be! Surely she can take exams at any time.'

Kite recognized that tone; it meant that Ruby was not expecting any further discussion.

'Of course I understand your feelings right at this moment, but you have to consider how this might affect her future,' Mr Scott answered not unkindly. He was such a tall imposing man that Kite had never noticed the surprisingly weak strain in his voice, especially when weighed against Ruby's.

'But she *has* a future, that's the point. And after what's happened to Dawn . . . We're not putting

58

any more pressure on her,' Ruby continued. She was adopting the 'stuck record method' that she had taught Kite to use in difficult situations. 'Just say the same thing over again in different ways, and eventually your message will get through,' Ruby had instructed her.

Seth must have passed Mr Scott in the doorway because their voices mingled together and fused with the drone of traffic from the street outside. There was silence for a while between Seth and Ruby. They were probably going through their ritual of hugging and kissing and comforting each other. Even though one of them was always off on tour, and they weren't even officially married, Ruby and Seth were probably the most 'together' couple of anyone's parents Kite knew.

Kite's mind flitted back to the day when she and Dawn had watched them snogging through a crack in the living-room door, and Dawn had laughed so hard that she'd almost wet herself!

'I don't think I've ever even seen my mum and dad kiss like that!' Dawn giggled.

Kite continued to listen through the wall. Her parents were sitting on the sofa that backed on to her bedroom wall, the sofa from which she had overheard so many of their 'secret' half-whispered conversations.

'What about this bereavement counsellor the doctor's set her up with?' Ruby asked.

'She's still refusing to go. Says she prefers to speak to Miss Choulty. I contacted the woman today about it and she says that we should keep a close eye on her, especially the not sleeping and eating, and definitely sign on with a local doctor as a temporary patient as soon as we get there. She's written a letter for us to take.'

'I suppose it's only for a few weeks, but she can't carry on like this with no sleep, Seth.'

'It's OK, Rubes, I know what to look out for. If it continues, or there's any sign of hallucinations, we'll have to take her to hospital and they might give her medication, but the doctor said that's always the last resort.'

'She doesn't need pills. She needs love and support and to talk it all through.' Ruby was crying.

'It's OK, Rubes. This counsellor, Lucy, says she'll talk to us too, all of us if it helps, and she'll see Kite any time when we get back for as long as she needs her for.'

'I'm thinking of cancelling my tour.'

'No need for that.' Seth sighed deeply. 'I'll look after her like I did when she was a baby.'

In the silence that followed, a feeling of outrage began to rise up in Kite. So they had made a plan to take her away somewhere without even consulting her. What did they think that she would do – follow in Dawn's footsteps? And if she couldn't talk to Miss Choulty, how was she going to speak to this counsellor? Never in a million years would she ever take her own life, but then again, the thought had never crossed her mind that Dawn would consider such a thing either.

Seth began strumming his guitar. He was playing her lullaby. The song that to thousands of other people was Seth Solomon's 'hit' belonged in truth only to her.

'It was your naming day that released the song writer in me,' he never tired of telling her.

She knew the words so well that she let them wash over her as she listened through the wall, the tune meandering through her thoughts.

'How do you see the world, my love?
Looking up at the sky
Eyes bright
Gazing into the blue
My love
Diamonds darting, lifting, floating . . .'

Tomorrow, Kite thought, I will be sixteen and it should be Dawn's turn to sit on my bed and wish me a happy birthday.

'Looking up at the sky
My love
Eyes bright
Hands unfolding, reaching out
So much hope
So much joy
So much life.'

Kite cast around the room, letting her eyes settle on the bright multicoloured diamonds of her birthday kites. There was no space for posters, or photos, or anything else apart from her long mirror, her wardrobe and a few bookshelves – because the fifteen kites, one for every year of her life, dominated her horizon. Just as well that even Ruby would understand there was no room now for any more kites after this year.

The door swung open gently, wafting kite tails. For a moment Kite almost expected Dawn to be standing there, but it was Seth who hovered in the entrance, strumming away, as if asking permission to enter. She nodded and he strolled around aimlessly; singing and playing, lost somewhere deep in his own thoughts.

Gradually, note by note, she felt her body relax. The song took her to a faraway time in her own childhood. Eventually Seth's voice trailed off. He placed his guitar by her bed and lay beside her. Tiredness swam around her head, and her eyelids felt unnaturally heavy. Seth flicked his sandy silver-flecked hair over one eye and fidgeted with his collection of leather bracelets. He had one from each of the many festivals he'd played at.

'I've been thinking that you and I should go away for the summer. Get away from . . . well – just get away really.'

When she didn't respond he continued. 'Sid from my record company's got this idea about a new ballad album. He's sending songwriters off to write about the places their ancestors came from.'

'Sheffield?'

'Your grandpa was from there, and your grandma was brought up in a children's home there, but it wasn't where she was from originally.' Kite nodded. She vaguely remembered him saying something about that, but as her grandparents had died before she was born, she never really felt that connected to them.

'Mum once told me that her maiden name, 'Storey', was from the Lake District or around that part of the world. When I was about your age I asked her why I didn't have any grandparents. She just said that her mum and dad had "given her up", she didn't know why and she didn't want to dwell on it. It was obviously too painful for her, so I stopped asking questions, but my finding out can't do her any harm now, can it? Besides, I've always wanted to see the Lakes; it's supposed to be beautiful up there.'

Kite was only half listening to Seth's ramblings, but she was grateful that he wasn't trying to get her to talk about Dawn or, worse still, her birthday. She had told Ruby a hundred times to cancel even the idea of it. She couldn't stand the thought of stepping into her seventeenth year without Dawn.

'Anyway I think it would be quite something for us to find out about my family's roots together,' Seth said in his soft, contemplative voice, still staring at the ceiling.

Ruby had been so set on teaching Kite about the history of her family in the Caribbean that Kite had spent most of her preschool years in St Kitts back when Grandad Cyril was alive. She could picture him holding on to her as she stood on his feet and he danced her around the room roaring with laughter. Ruby said that any daughter of hers should have carnival and sunshine in her soul. But all she knew about Seth's family is that they were from Sheffield, and now it seemed that even that was only half the story. It reminded Kite of something Dawn had said in drama one day, after Dawn's uncannily accurate impression of Ruby.

'I wish I came from somewhere else, like you!'

'But we're both from London!'

'Yes! But you know what I mean; you've got your St Kitts family too and all Ruby's arty connections. We don't really see anyone in our family. What do I say if someone asks me what my culture is?'

Now Kite thought she might be beginning to understand what Dawn had been getting at. Kite had Grandma Grace and Jai and all her cousins in St Kitts, and even though they were so far away, she Skyped them most weeks and they were always in her thoughts. So maybe if Dawn had belonged to a big bustling family of aunties and uncles and cousins, she might have found someone to talk to. Maybe if Dawn had had a Grandma Grace with all her funny stories . . . Now Kite thought about it, there were plenty of things that she might not tell Seth or Ruby, but she couldn't think of anything really that she would need to hide from her grandma.

On the occasions that he'd mentioned them, Seth always referred to his mother and father as 'Grandma Hannah' and 'Grandpa David', which was strange to Kite as Ruby and Seth always made such a big deal about people not being labelled by their titles.

'What was their surname?' Kite asked suddenly. When she spoke her voice sounded strangely flat and lifeless to her.

'Didn't I ever tell you?' Seth asked in surprise.

Kite shook her head.

'Jackson. I suppose I have found it a bit hard to talk about them – you know, because they died so close to when you were born. I was gutted about that. Your grandma went just a month before you arrived. Ruby was so pregnant at her funeral. That's what upset me the most. She was really looking forward to meeting you.' Seth's eyes filled with tears as he hugged Kite to him.

'I would have liked to meet her too. So I could have been Kite Jackson?' she asked as she tried out her new name. 'I prefer Solomon . . .'

Seth nodded. 'I did too! My "Song of Solomon" album did pretty well for me, so I never used Jackson after that! Anyway, what do you think to a road trip to the Lakes? How about setting off tomorrow? It might make it easier, on your birthday, to be doing something different.'

Kite shrugged by way of answer. She couldn't feel any worse than she already did, and maybe if she got away from Fairview and London, where everything reminded her of Dawn, she would be able to sleep.

'OK!' Kite whispered.

'Good!' Seth sighed with relief, wrapping his arm around Kite's shoulder. 'You know Ruby's choreographing this show in Manchester, so she can come up and visit from time to time. Wait till you see the house the record company's rented for us. It's supposed to have been designed by some prize-winning architect. Shall we have a look online?' Seth walked over to the computer and went to switch it on.

'Leave it, Seth,' Kite groaned.

'OK, then it can be a surprise.' He smiled, picked up his guitar and walked out of the room.

As soon as he was gone she regretted not showing more interest. He'd looked so upset when he'd talked about Grandma Hannah dying. Knowing Seth, he was probably trying to find a way to get her to share her grief with him, but she'd pushed him away, like she seemed to push everyone away now.

Bitter Sixteenth – 20 July

Kite watched as the display on her alarm clock switched to 5.42 a.m., the exact time of her birth. These were important times, times that people should know, the time of your birth and the time of your death, but even with the inquest over, nobody was able to pinpoint the moment of Dawn's death. With thoughts like these filling her mind, Kite was grateful to be heading off.

Kite watched the rain fall steadily. She couldn't remember the last time it had rained on her birthday. It had been raining since Dawn's funeral. It made her shudder now to think of Dawn, who had always smelt so clean, like a spring day, festering in the stagnant water of her grave. No! She would not allow these gruesome visions to enter her mind. Kite walked over to her bed and rested her head on her pillows, closed her eyes and tried to think of nothing.

*

No matter how long she lay there, just trying to breathe, she could not escape the endless whirring of her mind. She stood up, straightened her back and stretched out her arms as if she was walking a tightrope towards the mirror. Her breath misted the glass and it was a relief not to have to face herself on her most miserable birthday ever.

Kite crossed the room and logged on to Facebook. There were plenty of birthday messages from people in her tutor group. She quickly scrolled through them. There was a sweet one from Jamila – 'I'm thinking of you, and my family makes Dua for you every day. I've got a little present. Let me know when you're ready to see people.' There were also 'thinking of you's from the running club. 'Whenever you're ready to come back, we'll be waiting for you.' No one was insensitive enough to actually say 'Happy Birthday' but they sent their 'best wishes'. Next Kite read through the dozens of new messages on Dawn's memorial page. If she'd really been this popular, she would have had someone to talk to, thought Kite, closing down the screen and switching off her computer. *I don't ever want to read this rubbish again.* She was actually looking forward to getting in the car and driving away.

At that moment Ruby knocked on her door.

'Brought you some breakfast.'

The smell of freshly baked bread filled the flat. Usually, at the first wholesome scent of it, Kite's stomach would groan with hunger, but today it made her feel slightly sick. Ruby had put together a case of things that Kite might need: cagoules, sweatshirts, jumpers, outward-bound gear. 'You'll be grateful for this, because from what I hear, it always rains up there!' Ruby's voice was slightly strained and Kite tried not to meet her eyes – she knew her mother loved making a fuss of her on her birthday and she couldn't bear to hear anyone wish her happiness today.

'Got enough running gear?' asked Ruby, folding up a few Lycra tops and leggings from Kite's drawers and packing them in the case.

Kite didn't answer. Couldn't Ruby tell that she had no strength to walk, let alone run? It was as if she thought that running again would cure her. Of what? Dawn finishing herself off in her bedroom downstairs?

Ruby sat on the bed and wrapped her arms around her daughter's shoulders; the strength of her perfume made Kite cough. She pulled away sharply, but Ruby caught hold of her hand, refusing to let go.

'Let's just sit together, darlin', for a while. How about I do your nails, like we always do? Look! I've gone delicate turquoise; this is the exact colour of the blanket I wrapped you in when you were born!' She fluttered her fingers towards Kite.

Kite flinched.

'Sorry. I'm not in the mood.'

69

'I know you don't want me to, but I think it's wrong not to at least mark your sixteenth birthday. There's only one thing I have to give to you.'

'Why can't you just leave me alone?' Kite's voice was shrill and full of anger.

'You know this is hard for all of us.' Kite noticed that her mother's eyes were bloodshot as she looked back at her from the doorway. Seth always said that Ruby was warm enough to break the iciest heart, and at that moment Kite realized how selfish she was being: it was Ruby who needed to mark her birthday, more than she did. She reminded herself how much she regretted being so off with Seth yesterday and relented.

'OK,' she sighed. 'Bring it through!'

For sixteen years this moment had been just between the two of them. Ruby reappeared in the doorway, her hands behind her back, unable to hide the size of her diamond-shaped parcel. Kite felt nothing inside, not the usual bubbling up of excitement, or the ridiculous urgency she'd always felt as soon as she held the new kite in her hands; to run with it and watch it soar through the sky. Since Dawn had moved into Fairview her ritual had been to call for her to fly her kite with her on her birthday morning.

'Come on, darlin'.' Ruby laid a hand on Kite's arm as she listlessly unwrapped the first layer of bright yellow tissue paper.

In front of her was a kite unlike any of the others in her collection. She ran her fingers over what looked like a patchwork of tiny triangular pieces of parachute silk. Handwritten into each coloured panel in gold and silver were birthday wishes from people from all parts of her life, here and in St Kitts. Ruby's sparkling fingernails traced over the many messages that she must have spent weeks collecting and sewing together.

'Happy Birthday, my beauty,' read the message from Grandma Grace.

'Go crazy, girl!' her cousin Jai wrote, in his so-laid-back-it-was-almost-lying-down, spidery handwriting.

On one triangle was written: 'To our wonderful daughter, our Kite Spirit, on your 16th birthday, love Ruby and Seth xx'.

Ruby hugged her tight as she read her own message and for a moment Kite closed her eyes and allowed herself to be comforted.

'There are loads more messages,' Ruby encouraged her, and for her mother's sake only Kite opened her eyes and read on.

'You turn my world! Love Mali xxx'

'Who's Mali?' Ruby asked, smiling as she read the message at the same time as Kite. 'I sent a few triangles and pens in a packet down to Circus Space and this is what came back.' Well, they *had* been sort of going out together – 'sort of' was actually the only way she had ever been out with a boy. It didn't seem worth spending so much time with someone unless you really cared and, the truth is, she had never felt that way about anyone yet.

'Just someone at Circus Space,' she muttered.

Reading this now, she wondered what Mali thought of her for not being in touch; he'd been messaging her on Facebook and she just hadn't replied. She'd let her phone run out of charge ages ago because she couldn't stand to see Dawn's name on it. What do you do with the text messages from your best friend when she's not here any more? Deleting them would be like erasing her. Anyway, Kite hadn't seen any recent messages from Mali – no birthday wishes on Facebook this morning – so she assumed that he had finally given up on her.

Kite read on.

'We have an appointment on the cloud swing! Love Annalisa x'

Ruby attempted to skip the next message, gliding over it. But the second that Kite recognized the careful handwriting, she moved Ruby's hand aside to reveal . . .

'Happy Birthday, "Thithter". Here's to flying for your 16th! Love Dawn X'

'I got everyone to sign the silk ages ago so that I'd have time to sew it together,' explained Ruby.

It was all too much for Kite.

'All history now.' She spat the bitter words at Ruby.

72

'I thought about taking Dawn's message out, but that didn't feel right either . . .'

They sat in silence for a while. 'Thank you,' Kite whispered, softening as she took in the work that Ruby must have put into making this. She squeezed Ruby's hand before getting up and walking around the room to examine her collection of kites. A different colour for every year, but there was nothing that came close to this exquisite hand-made multicoloured creation.

'The material's from recycled carnival costumes.' Ruby smoothed her hands over the silk. 'Well, you know, my darlin', it was meant to be such a special birthday.' Her liquid liner had smudged with tears, leaving dark rings around her eyes like bruises.

'I'm on the phone any time of the day or night if you need me, and I'll come over when I can.' Ruby smiled.

'I'm not taking my mobile,' Kite mumbled.

'I never thought I'd hear the day!' Ruby took Kite's chin in her hands, and Kite pulled away from her once more. 'Well, Seth's got his, so we can always talk. I know how tired you are, darlin' – maybe you'll sleep in the car.' Ruby clapped her palms against her head as if she'd been a fool. 'I can't believe I didn't think of that before. It's how we used to get you to sleep when you were a baby . . . driving you around the block.'

'Don't you get it? Little Kite's not a baby any more,

and little Dawn's—' She stopped abruptly.

Ruby didn't deserve any of her outbursts, but when Kite spoke to her like this it felt as if she had no idea how grown up her daughter had become.

The doorbell rang – a single, hesitant ring.

Ruby sighed deeply and walked out of the room. She was always being called on by someone, for something. She felt that neighbours should know each other, help each other out, like family. Whenever there was a Fairview block party, it would always be Ruby hosting it, and hanging bunting from the little communal walkways. It had been Ruby's idea to paint each of the front doors a different 1930s colour, in keeping with the period of the building, with its large leaded windows and simple red brick. People walking along the street below would look up and admire or frown at the acid-green, the creamy orange, light turquoise and salmon-pink doors. Dawn's door (it would always be Dawn's door to Kite) was salmon pink and looked especially lovely this summer with Hazel's planting of delicate sweet peas. Kite often used to think how much each door suited its inhabitants. Her own was of the brightest orange with a large blue glazed pot at the entrance, like a Caribbean sky. Out of the pot grew long-necked birds of paradise with their magnificent orange and purple crests. As Ruby never tired of telling her, Kite had been born in this flat, and so it had always been home for her. Now that had been spoilt too. Kite wondered if she would ever be able to rid her mind of the vile image of her friend lying alone as she stood outside her door and knocked and knocked.

Kite could hear by the soft lilt in Ruby's voice that she was comforting someone. A lemon smell wafted into her room, reminding her so much of Dawn that she found herself being drawn out of her bedroom. Maybe she really had come back and it had all been a terrible dream, a nightmare that she had finally woken up from. But there, standing in the hallway, was Hazel, in the exact same place that Dawn had so often stood. Even though she only lived on the landing below, it was the first time Kite had seen her since the funeral. She had always been thin, but now the skin hollowed over her cheekbones, and the deep indents under her eyes made her look as if she was half starving. She was clasping Dawn's Raggedy Anne doll in her hands. She looked up at Kite with her watery hazel eyes that were the same delicate colour as Dawn's. Kite attempted to pull her face muscles into something like a smile. With the effort she bit her bottom lip so hard that she drew blood.

'You smell of Dawn,' Kite whispered, walking towards her.

Hazel nodded, as if it was the most normal thing to say in the world. 'I've been using her soap. It makes me feel closer to her.'

Ruby stared from Hazel to Kite as if she was afraid to break into their conversation.

'I heard you're going away,' Hazel murmured.

Kite nodded. She would have liked to say something to comfort Hazel, but what could be said or done now? Her mind drifted back to the day in Year 1 when Dawn had told her that she was moving flat. Then a removal van had appeared in the courtyard below. Ruby and Kite had popped down with tea and home-made muffins to find that it was Dawn Jenkins moving in, and they had giggled till they cried to find that they, who were already inseparable, were to be neighbours!

'Now we really are like thithters!' Dawn joked, even though, by then she had lost her lisp.

Ruby placed an arm around Hazel's narrow shoulders and steered her towards the sofa. 'I'll make us some tea,' she soothed as she went through to the kitchen.

'I made her tea in a flask and left a croissant on the table for her breakfast,' whispered Hazel. 'You see, I was on the early shift and Jimmy was on nights and he was coming in just after school time. He was hoping to get back earlier, but it was all over by then anyway.' Hazel was rocking gently in her seat, clasping the doll in her lap as if it was a baby. Kite wasn't even sure she was talking to her. 'When the school called me to say she hadn't arrived, I told them I'd set out her uniform all washed and ironed, and her breakfast – you know I always leave a good breakfast . . . and a new pencil case with the fine tip pens in . . . she says . . . she said . . . made her writing the neatest, and a little good-luck card because God help me, I didn't want to wake her.' Her voice cracked.

Kite leaned forward in her seat, searching desperately for something kind to say to Hazel, whose hands were now clasped tight to her face. The skin on her hands and arms was rubbed raw and her eczema had opened into bloody cracks between her fingers.

'It's true, you always left breakfast for her,' was the only thing Kite could think of to say, but her words seemed to calm Hazel down.

'I'm sorry, love; I came to wish you well, not upset you.' Hazel took a deep breath to compose herself again. 'I've been going through Dawn's things,' she whispered, placing her hand in her jacket pocket, 'and I found this.' She handed Kite a sealed white envelope. 'It's your birthday card!' Hazel's voice sounded strange and distant. She looked down at her sore hands and Kite watched as she clasped and unclasped the cracked tips of her fingers. 'It was under her pillow, and I'm afraid we had to open it. With all of this autopsy business, the police said she might have left a message for you. Anyway, it turns out it's just a birthday card. I thought you should have it!'

This was what made Kite feel worse than anything: the sense that when people looked at her they thought that she might hold some of the clues to why Dawn had done what she did. If Dawn had confided in her, did they think she would have kept it to herself? She heard it in all the questions she was asked . . . in Ruby's 'If there's anything, I mean *anything*, you want to talk about . . .' In Miss Choulty's kindly 'You are not to blame for anything'. And now, worst of all, she read it in the searchlight questioning of Hazel's eyes. Kite held her hand out for the card and for a moment Hazel kept hold of the envelope, as if she was reluctant to let go.

'We also found a letter from the conductor who came to the funeral. It was addressed to me and Jimmy, but I suppose Dawn must have hidden it. It said how the conductor wanted to have a meeting with us all. It was a kind letter, you know. What was it he said? That she wasn't just good, she was "extraordinary". They wanted her back as their top oboe. I can't understand why she hid it from us.'

Kite nodded, but she felt as if she should find a way of telling Hazel what she felt to be true. Music wasn't just a hobby to Dawn. It was her way of speaking . . . and once she had stopped playing, she had stopped speaking too. Sitting here with Hazel, it felt like a mistake to be going away at all. It seemed that the only people who would really understand what was going on inside her were Hazel and Jimmy. Hazel spoke about Dawn as if she was still here too; she couldn't bring herself to place her in the past either.

Hazel lowered her eyes as she finally released the card from her grip. Kite's name had been written in Dawn's best italic ink pen. She turned it over to find the neatly resealed edges of the envelope and lifted it to her nose. It smelt of Dawn.

Ruby walked in with a tray of mugs, and Kite swiftly took the card and placed it in her bag.

'Let's be off!' shouted Seth, bounding up the steps. 'Where's your stuff? The car's all packed!' He was freshly shaven and had put on his favourite blue denim shirt and beaten-up suede jacket. He was wearing some new linen trousers and the leather Converse Ruby had bought him for his birthday the week before. As soon as he saw Hazel he slowed his pace, walked over to her and clasped her hand in his.

'Sorry, I didn't know you were visiting.'

'Have some tea,' intercepted Ruby, handing him a mug.

Hazel took a sip and placed the mug back on the table.

'And I was wondering, is there anything you want of hers?' murmured Hazel without looking up.

Kite's mind went blank. What possession of Dawn's could give her real comfort now? Hazel raised her hand to the plain silver cross she wore around her own neck and that sparked an idea.

'Maybe the locket I bought her?'

'She's still wearing that,' Hazel said.

Actually Kite was relieved to hear they hadn't taken the locket off Dawn. As far as she knew, she had worn it every day since she'd given it to her in Year 6. And now she thought of it there was something else of Dawn's that she would like to hold close.

'I'd like . . . the little box I gave her for her birthday, with her reeds in, and if I could just listen to her iPod?' It sounded like an odd request even to Kite, but somehow she felt that if she could only listen to Dawn's music she might be able to sleep again.

'Of course. We don't know what to do with all her oboe things – sheet music and everything. Jimmy thinks we should give it to the school, so someone else gets to play. Are you sure that's *all* you want?'

Kite nodded.

'OK, well, I must be off. We're packing up ourselves. We asked for an emergency move. The council's been very understanding actually. I just wanted to wish you . . . well, if Dawn had been here we would have seen you on your birthday . . .'

'Poor, poor woman,' sighed Ruby as they listened to her walk down the stairs.

A part of Kite wanted to rip up the card. What was the point of it anyway? It's not as if Dawn had cared enough to confide in her. She didn't want Dawn's beautiful writing or her words haunting her from beyond the grave. She just wanted Dawn back and everything to be how it was before.

The Angel of the North

Ruby stood on the pavement waving them off. In the car, Kite lowered her head as some students in her year walked past chatting and laughing on their way into school. It felt wrong that the world was going on just as it always had. At the far end of the road she spotted the familiar face of the postman working his way up the street. A removal van had double-parked, and Jimmy was loading Dawn's little blue bedroom sofa into it. How many times had they come in from school and slumped down on that? Jimmy caught Kite staring at him, dug his hand deep in his pocket and came over to the car.

'Hazel says you wanted these,' he muttered, handing her a gift bag through the half-open car window. Kite looked inside to find the tiny leather reed box, Dawn's iPod and three bars of lemon soap.

'Well, I'll be seeing you then.' Jimmy tapped on the side window, lowered his head and started making his way back towards Fairview. Before Kite knew what was happening, Seth had flung open his door, leaving the car stranded in the middle of the road, and jumped out.

'Wait up!'

Jimmy stood frozen with his back towards Seth, who took hold of his broad shoulders and turned him around. As far as she could see the two men said nothing at all. They just stood in the pouring rain holding each other. Jimmy clung on to Seth so tightly that his knuckles turned white.

Back in the car, Seth took off his sodden jacket and waved to Ruby one last time, slammed the door and revved the engine. Kite stared into the rear-view mirror and saw the postman hand a small package to Ruby. She signed for it, then read the label, raised her hand in the air, shaking it wildly, and came hurtling towards the car.

'Wait up! Wait!'

Seth, who had almost negotiated his way around the removal van, slammed on the brakes.

'What is it now?' he groaned.

'You can't go without this!' Ruby panted, handing the package to Kite through her window. 'It's from Grandma Grace; she was desperate for you to have it on your birthday.'

Ruby held her daughter's chin for a moment, then turned quickly. Kite saw her lift her hands to her eyes as she walked away.

'She misses Grace so much, you know,' Seth

explained, turning to Kite as he pulled away. 'I can't even begin to imagine how Jimmy and Hazel are going to carry on. Sorry I haven't been able to write your song, just haven't felt up to it . . . but maybe once we're in the Lakes.'

Along with money to go shopping with, the kite and the song had been her birthday presents for as long as she could remember. It was always the same: the kite from Ruby and the song from Seth. She had never wanted anything different, but she was glad that Seth had not been able to write anything this year. There was nothing to sing about now anyway.

'What did Grace send you then?' asked Seth as he peered down at the envelope that lay on Kite's lap beside Dawn's reed box.

Kite unpeeled the Sellotape. Inside was a small black box. She lifted the lid to find Grandma Grace's precious rose-gold St Christopher in her hand.

'I never thought she'd part with that!' Seth whistled.

Kite felt around in the envelope and found a little notelet.

Sweet darlin',
My heart aches with sadness for you. I'm here anytime you want, if you need a shoulder to cry on. Maybe between us we can get the money together for your visit. The sunshine would help to heal you. If not, I will try to come to you soon.

83

Never mind if you don't believe – after what has happened to that poor child, I would like you to wear this for me, my sweet girl. It would make me happy to feel you safe.

You know you have all my love, and no matter how far away I am, or what trouble life brings, I will always be with you in spirit.

Your cousins send you all their love,

Your Grandma Grace.

Kite opened the little catch and placed the chain around her neck. The small pendant lay flat against her chest. It felt good to be wearing something sent from St Kitts. She could picture her grandma sitting on her chair outside her beach house, feet planted in the sand, admiring the waves and the setting sun as was her evening ritual.

Dawn opened the second box to find a single reed nestling in the middle groove of the moulded green velvet. She recognized the golden thread that Dawn had tied around the reed to mark that it had been her best one yet. It had taken Kite a long time to understand exactly what went into this reed-making ritual, but somehow the ceremony and the perfection of it all seemed to fit Dawn's personality.

'If I were you I'd keep all of them, so I could say, "This is the reed I was using when I played my first concert," or, "This is the reed I was using when I got into my music school . . ." You could tell your life story through your reed collection. First-kiss reed, First day at Uni reed . . .' Kite joked.

'It's not like that.' Dawn laughed. 'Once it's let you down you never trust it again, so you don't want to keep it, but this one's different.' Dawn held up the golden reed. 'I'll keep this, because even though it's all worn out, it's never let me down. Anyway, this is the one you saw me play at the Brahms concert.'

Kite stared down at the delicate reed. Dawn had always been the one to think deeply about things, to weigh her words carefully. All these glowering thoughts that had started gathering in Kite's mind since the Falling Day were new to her. The truth was that until now she had never thought that deeply about anything. Never curbed the things she'd said either, and this directness was what had always made Dawn laugh. She turned the worn bamboo over in her hands; it reminded her of a tiny oar. If this little reed really could speak to her now, what sad, desperate music would it play? She placed it back inside the leather box and closed the lid. Then she reached into the bag that Jimmy had given her, took out a bar of soap and unwrapped it slowly. What an odd collection of things she found herself clinging on to. She closed her eyes and breathed in the lemon scent.

'I'm going to try to get some sleep!' Kite announced as Seth switched on a CD.

'Got the perfect music for you then!'

It was one of his band's folk tracks. She'd always quite liked it but listening to him singing along to it now it irritated her. The world is not full of sweet harmonies, Kite thought as she watched the wipers swish back and forth across the windscreen.

'Mind if I climb into the back?' asked Kite, but Seth was miles away, lost in his own thoughts and concentrating on the road. So she took off her seat belt and clambered over. Ruby had covered the fraying upholstery with a blanket and placed a pillow and her duvet on top. This comfy little nest spoke of a cosy time when fresh bedding, a warm cup of sweetened milk and a hot water bottle could make her feel like all was well with the world.

The heavy spray from the road splattered the side windows as she plugged in her earphones and began listening to Dawn's iPod. The first track was something classical and discordant that she had never heard before; she flicked forward and there playing in her ear was Brahms's Symphony No. 1 that she had come to know off by heart, especially Dawn's solos. She imagined that Dawn was practising in her bedroom and she was listening to her playing through the walls. She tucked a bar of soap under the pillow, closed her eyes, wrapped her hands around the reed box and let the music wash over her, feeling the weight and warmth of Grandma Grace's gift against her skin.

'Shh, shh, sleep now, child, listen to that English rain wash it all away my darlin', wash it away.'

Kite followed Dawn's oboe into the music, meandering along the pure smooth notes, and the rain fell and fell.

I am staring down into a deep puddle and the water gathers and swells and spreads across the land until I am standing on the edge of a huge river. The waves rise high and the wind roars. Out of the waves steps a man, a giant man who turns to me with gentle grey eyes.

'Are you looking for your friend?'

I don't answer him, but place my feet in the water and, as I do, a flotilla of tiny bamboo reed boats floats towards me.

Now I'm sitting on a boardwalk, placing my bare feet into the cold, cold water.

'You must stay on the shore,' the giant warns me.

I lean down and try to scoop up all the reeds, but I can't hold on to them; they slip through my fingers and I have to start all over again.

'Are you looking for your friend?' the giant asks again, and he lowers his body down into the water and re-emerges carrying a girl on his shoulders. He turns away from me and wades her across the river.

'Dawn!' I cry after her, but she is slumped over his shoulder and she doesn't lift her head.

'Walk along a river with me,' he calls beckoning me to follow . . .

'Walk along a river.' Seth's voice was . . . calling her back.

Kite's head knocked against the hard plastic panelling of the car door. Her mind was thick with a dream-fog so heavy it took her several blinks to remember where she was. Cautiously she opened her eyes to find that the rain had cleared, revealing a watery blue sky. Kite stared at Seth. As he sang, tears streamed down his face. Maybe he felt her watching him, because he half turned towards her. She clamped her eyes shut as if she was in a deep sleep. It felt wrong to have witnessed him crying like that.

She was desperate to get back into the dream, no matter how weird it had been. It was so long since she'd experienced anything more than a fleeting sleep. The game Ruby had played with her and Dawn when they'd first camped out at a festival filled Kite's head.

'Close your eyes and open your senses,' Ruby ordered them as they lay underneath the bright blue canopy of their tent, Ruby snuggling up to them both.

Ruby had made it up for Dawn's benefit. They had been nine years old then, but as long as she'd known her Dawn had always been afraid of the dark.

'Listen! What can you hear?' Ruby said.

At first Dawn had jumped at every rustle of the earth until Ruby had gone through each sound and identified it. A squirrel skittering through the leaves, the hoot of an owl, a car door slamming, the patter of rain on canvas and eventually Ruby's voice had faded away as they drifted into sleep.

Kite closed her eyes and listened to Seth singing and the cars and lorries speeding past on the wet road . . .

I'm in the flat dancing. There is a loud knock at the door and then someone rings the bell over and over. I turn down the radio and look at the clock. I can't believe it's already so late.

It's Dawn standing in the doorway, half scowling at me.

'How can you be late on the day of your first exam?'

'Sorry! Just got to find my shoes,' I call back to her, rummaging around in the front room, grabbing my bag and a piece of toast off the table and slamming the door behind me.

Dawn runs down the steps, grabs a bunch of sweet peas and hands them to me as I catch up with her. 'For luck!' she smiles.

'I'm going to need it,' I say. At the bottom of the steps Jess runs across the road to greet us.

'There you go! A black cat crossing your path – isn't that supposed to be good luck?' I laugh, reaching out for her arm, but there is no one there.

'Dawn!' I call into the empty street.

Jess is at my feet, arching her back and miaowing louder and louder until she's hissing and snarling, sticking her claws deep into my ankles.

'Hey, Kite!' Seth was shouting, turning around. 'You're kicking the back of my seat.'

Kite opened her eyes to see Seth holding his mobile

in one hand. She stared out of the window at an open green field with horses grazing. They'd pulled over on to a grass verge.

'No, no, she's fine, Rubes. Slept all the way up here. I can't believe it . . . We'll have to find another way to get her to sleep though – this old banger won't stand too much more of a battering! It's Ruby calling to see how you're doing,' he told Kite, raising the phone back up to his ear. 'OK, I'll tell her . . . don't worry,' he reassured her before hanging up. 'Ruby's going into rehearsals now, but she'll call back later.' Seth smiled at Kite as he pulled away from the verge and continued slowly down a gravel track. 'Just a bit of a detour!'

Kite's eyes were so heavy that it felt as if she'd been drugged. She propped herself up on her elbows and stared out of the window at a huge steel structure . . . a kind of giant with great welcoming wings. The top of her head felt bruised from knocking against the side of the car. She decided not to tell Seth about her dreams. He was big on interpreting them, and the last thing she needed now was for him to start analysing what was going on in her head.

'Remember you said last year you wanted to see this. I know it can't be a happy birthday but . . . !' Seth broke off mid-sentence, opened his door and swung Kite's side open too. She got out, leaned her back against the sun-warmed metal of the bonnet and stared up at the steel wingspan.

'The Angel of the North against a bright blue sky!' Seth picked up a leaflet that someone had discarded on the ground and read. 'Says here, it's the height of four double-decker buses, with the girth of a jumbo jet!'

As they strolled in the sunshine up the grassy slope, Kite had the feeling that she was attending some sort of ritual ceremony. There were people walking their dogs and tiny children running as if into the arms of the angel. Only a few weeks ago Kite would have run like that too, but now she could hardly walk a few paces without feeling disorientated. At the top of the hill, a young couple in matching red leather biker jackets were locked in a kiss.

Seth walked away a little and lay down on the grass directly under the angel.

'I've been watching the forecast. It's hard to believe with the wet weather we've been having in London, but it looks like there's been no rain here for weeks,' he said as he patted the yellowing grass for Kite to sit down next to him. Then he unpacked the feast that Ruby had prepared the night before. She had made up her usual stack of silver tiffin tins.

'I thought a picnic was a cheese sandwich, maybe a sausage roll and a bag of crisps!'

Dawn had been amazed the first time she'd tasted one of Ruby's picnics.

As Seth opened the containers, the smell of jerk

chicken and home-made patties wafted around the feet of the angel. The kissing couple sniffed the air and pulled apart.

'Ah! The power of Ruby's cooking!' Seth laughed.

Kite felt not even the slightest whisper of hunger, but she took a tiny mouthful.

'She's made your favourite cake too!'

'I told her not to bother,' Kite grumbled, pushing the basket of food away from her. It was all wrong. Here she was with her dad sitting in this amazing place eating one of Ruby's ridiculously over-the-top picnics while Jimmy was packing Dawn's things away on to a removal van. I wonder what he's done with the chair that she tied her reeds on, thought Kite. Every time Dawn tied a reed she would leave a little silken thread attached, like a collection of friendship bracelets on a wrist.

Seth brought out a small chocolate and cinnamon cake wrapped in silver foil. In the centre he placed a single candle and lit it with his lighter.

'Thought you'd given up?' Kite sighed.

'I have . . . had . . . until all this! Never mind that now! Ruby thought you might want to make a wish for Dawn.'

'OK, why not?' said Kite, trying not to feel angry at Ruby again. Scrunching her eyes closed, she wished harder than she had ever done for anything that she could see Dawn again. She opened her eyes and pursed her lips to blow the candle out, but just at that moment there was a gust of wind. It lifted Kite's hair so that it streamed on the air behind her, and the flickering flame blew out.

'Shall I light it again?' Seth offered.

'What's the point?' Kite sighed.

'Is it a building or a sculpture?' asked Kite, staring up at the rust-coloured steel.

Seth shrugged. Whatever it was, she was glad that the angel had an armour of steel to protect it from the weather. She wondered how you set about building the foundations for such a mammoth structure.

'Do you think it'll ever fall?' she asked Seth as she stared up at it.

'Hope not! If it did, it would crush everything in its path, that's for sure.'

'No chance of that!' answered a thickset balding man, catching their conversation as he passed. 'Helped to build those foundations with my own hands. It's more likely to fly than fall!' he joked as he linked arms with a stooped old lady.

'We'll be begging her for rain before the summer's out! I've never known such a dry run,' the lady remarked, her pale green headscarf billowing in the breeze. It seemed cruel the way that she had to distort her spine in order to look up at the sky but, from the look of awe on her face, she clearly thought it worth the effort. 'And to think that you had a part in her making!' she sighed contentedly.

'I've told you, Mam, he's a *man* of steel, a proper Geordie shipbuilding angel!'

'To you maybe!' The old woman laughed.

Their voices faded as they made their way back down the slope.

'She reminded me of your Grandma Hannah,' Seth told her. 'Funny! She always wore a little chiffon headscarf too.'

Kite turned to him and caught the emotion in his eyes.

'You know my dad was her man of steel, worked on the railways as an engineer. She was as proud of your grandad as that old woman of her son.'

Kite nodded and stared up at the giant angel again. 'What's it meant to symbolize?'

Seth took Kite's hand in his and stared up with her. 'I dunno, but it's genius, isn't it? To build something that weighs tonnes, but that you truly believe could step off the hillside and fly.'

He paused for a moment and flicked his hair away from his eyes. 'Something about seeing all this, after all that's happened . . .'

Everyone had their own way of avoiding the S word. Seth's preferred phrase was 'all that's happened'.

'I don't know how to explain it, Kite, but this

94

sculpture is stirring me up. I know what it is! It gets you here,' he said, punching his own chest. 'It's like there's something hopeful in its gut . . .'

How could he talk of 'hope'? At this moment she wished she could have been packed into Jimmy and Hazel's removal van and gone to live with them; at least they wouldn't have tried to distract her, to take her out of herself, and one thing she knew for sure, they definitely would not have talked of hope. It had been the worst idea of all to come away, because now all she felt was guilty to be here, in this place, under a picture-book sky that seemed to trample on her feelings. She had preferred the rain.

'If there's so much hope in the world, why did Dawn give up on everything?'

Seth shook his head, staring up at the angel as if this steel structure could hold the answer to her question. There was a time when Kite had believed that Seth held the answers to everything. A part of her wished she could go back there, to that time when a good kite-flying day, a blue sky and a gust of wind would mean nothing but happiness.

Part Two
Lost

Lost

The grey road seemed to stretch on forever. Kite wasn't sure when it had happened exactly, but there came a moment when she realized they were surrounded by mountains, and then she knew for sure that agreeing to come into this perfect pastoral fantasy had been a mistake. Cows grazed in the fields close to the roads, and far away the hillside was dotted with what resembled clusters of white flowers swaying in the wind.

'When I was your age, I had this romantic vision of myself as a shepherd!' Seth smiled, following her gaze up to the distant sheep.

Staring out at the endless green she really couldn't believe that she'd let herself be talked into coming. What was she going to DO here? The house they were staying in was apparently in the middle of nowhere. Now she thought about it, she'd never really spent much time in the countryside just for the sake of it. Camping at festivals in Devon and Cornwall or Suffolk didn't really count, because they were always swarming with people, activity and life. The countryside had been somewhere they'd gone to for a reason, like outward-bound trips to Wales with school – and for years now Dawn had always been by her side.

'Looks like we're going to be lucky with the weather.' Seth opened the window and held out his hand to feel the warm air. 'I remember watching a film about two jokers coming up here from London and it rained so much that they ended up walking around with bin bags on their feet! Come to think of it, I watched that film on my first date with Rubes. I didn't really fancy it, but I fancied Rubes so I went along and it was actually laugh-out-loud funny. I'll have to get it out for you when we get up there. There's no TV, but they're bound to have a computer and screen to watch films on.'

'Why no TV?'

'It's a complete getaway. We'll have to make our own entertainment.'

Great! She wouldn't even be able to escape from her own thoughts, let alone block Seth out. His constant attempts to cheer her up already made her feel like flinging open the car door and running away.

They were driving through a small town now with a clock tower made of sandstone at the centre. A group of boys and girls about her age was hanging out on the wide steps that led up to the tower. Strewn around the bottom were bikes, a cluster of mopeds and one beaten-up old motorbike. One of the girls, with shocking pink hair and an impressive collection of ear studs and a nose-ring, glanced into the car and smiled at Kite.

Seth pulled up in front of an old-fashioned delicatessen. Now some of the boys, sharing a bag of chips, were glancing over at her too.

'Come on, let's stretch our legs,' Seth said, jumping out of the car.

'I'll wait here,' she muttered.

The smell of cold meats and strong cheeses wafted towards her through the open window, making her feel sick. Anyway, there was no way she was getting out of the car with that lot staring at her.

After a while the group of teenagers got on their various bikes and headed off in different directions. The girl with pink hair climbed on the back of the motorbike and the oldest-looking boy, wearing a badge-covered leather jacket, started revving the cranky-sounding engine. The girl turned and nodded in Kite's direction as she secured her helmet.

After they had left, Kite watched people coming and going from the deli. They seemed to be watching her too. A lot of them were quite old; some so old that they seemed to have to stop every step just to catch their breath. From the way they looked at her, she wondered whether they could tell that something awful had happened to her. Or maybe there was another reason. Now she thought of it, nobody she'd seen in the town, except for the Chinese woman she'd spotted coming out of the restaurant, had been anything else but white. Everyone in London was from different backgrounds, and most of the time she never thought about being 'black' or 'mixed-race' – or what was it that Ruby came back from a job in America saying half-jokingly? – 'a person of colour'. In fact Dawn sometimes said in London that *she* felt the odd one out for *not* being from somewhere else. At home Kite would have just been a girl sitting in a car, but here she attracted attention. She should never have come.

Then, as if to contradict her, a young woman walked past, struggling on to the pavement with a double buggy. Seth was coming out of a shop and Kite watched him offer to help. He leaned down to the children and ruffled their hair. They were twin girls with skin the colour of Kite's and tangly wild hair. Seth pointed in Kite's direction, and the young mother looked up at her and nodded. Seth came jogging over to the car, his backpack full of groceries.

'Did you see those sweet little girls? They reminded me of you when you were a toddler. Sorry I was so long. People do like to chat around here. I can tell you, they're a friendly lot,' Seth gabbled on as he started up the car.

Sometimes she sensed that Seth wished she was still that sweet little girl.

'All right?'

Kite nodded. Maybe she'd been hasty to assume that she was completely in the minority here. She smiled as they passed a minibus with 'Birmingham City Challenge' written on the side. It could have been an outing from her own school, with black and Asian kids and a few white kids in there too. Kite had the ridiculous impulse to wave at them. What was going on with her? At home these thoughts would never have crossed her mind. She supposed it was because for the first time in her life she felt like an outsider. That's how Dawn said she felt all the time in her orchestra. Like she didn't fit and maybe like she didn't even have the right to be there.

They were winding along a country lane, following a sign that read: 'To the heart of the Lakes'. Kite recognized some of the place names from streets she knew in London: 'Coniston', 'Windermere' and 'Buttermere'.

Seth pulled over to switch on the satnav he'd bought especially for this journey and listened for a moment.

'Does she seem bossy to you?' he grimaced as the nasal-sounding satnav woman ordered them down narrower and narrower lanes. Seth insisted on reading out the names of all the villages they passed in the early-evening sunshine.

'Drybeck . . . Eskdale . . . Longsleddale . . . we're in the land of the Celts and Vikings now!' he declared.

To Kite these places sounded like they belonged to a different country and time.

Now they were entering 'Swindale Common' and had slowed to cross a cattle grid. When they were halfway over, a herd of sheep ambled in front of them, forcing them to stop. Seth wound his window down.

'Evening,' he said to the sheep.

One of them stopped and looked at him idly for a second and then wandered on.

'Smell that!' he ordered Kite as he stuck his head out of his window and breathed in the fresh, clean mountain air.

Kite frowned. She gazed out of the window, her eyes following the path of a stream that ran alongside the road, scrambling over rocks and tumbling into deeper pools.

'I've had enough of you "Boss-Nav"!' Seth switched off the engine and cut her off mid-command. 'I'm not about to be in the most beautiful place in the world and be ordered about by you!'

He got out of the car, stretched and wandered down to the stream. A little way off some dishevelled-looking fell ponies stared at them before turning and trotting off. If Dawn was here, she would probably have thought it was the most beautiful place in the world too.

'A penny for them?' Seth asked, peering into the car and holding out his hand.

'You wouldn't want to know.'

'Well, we're in the wilds now!' Seth announced as Kite reluctantly followed him along the stream. She took off her shoes and dangled her feet in the icy water. A flash of Kite's dream in the car returned to her and she felt as if she'd been here before, desperately trying to gather up Dawn's floating reeds. Seth lay down on a flat rock and stared up at the fading blue sky.

'Listen to the music of the mountain stream . . .' he sang. 'Scrap that! Corny, isn't it?'

Kite nodded and half smiled. As she did, a rusty green tractor grumbled towards them along the track. A boy of about her age, maybe a bit older, was driving. Lydia in her tutor group had written something random this morning on her Facebook page: 'Congratulations, now you can drive a tractor! As if!' Seth sat up and the boy nodded towards him and raised his hand in a friendly wave, then his eyes moved over to Kite and a warm smile spread across his face as he continued to wave to her, as if he recognized her. His eyes sparkled grey like the slate of the mountain, his sandy-blond hair was cut short, his skin all weather-tanned. Kite played with her hair, teasing the curls over her scar.

'Looks like you caught someone's eye.' Seth grinned at her.

'Shut up, Seth!' Kite snapped. It was bad enough that, just for a moment, she had been so mesmerized by the boy. How could she even think about fancying someone so soon after . . . How shallow did that make her? Kite felt the muscles tense and she forced herself to wipe the stupid smile from her face and purse her lips closed. This was a new feeling and the worst yet, when just for a second she forgot what had happened. If Dawn had been here, that boy would have provided them with hours of gossip, wondering who he was, where he came from, which one of them would stand a chance. If Dawn had been here, he might have smiled at her too, but now that would never happen. Seeing this boy made her understand why she felt so angry. Dawn had robbed Kite of sharing the stories of her life – funny stories, sad stories, love stories, predictable stories, mistakes and successes with her best friend. Dawn's was a story not even half written.

'Seriously though, I think this place is going to be good for both of us.' Seth sighed with pleasure. There it was again, his favourite topic – the healing power of the countryside.

'I just wish we could have come here with your Grandma Hannah.'

Kite had only been vaguely listening when Seth had started talking about tracing his family history, but now she realized how revved up about it he really was. At least if he gets caught up in that he might leave me alone, she thought as she stood up and meandered along the stream, using her hands to steady herself over the uneven boulders. If Miss Choulty was here she would be waxing lyrical about this glacial scenery – rocks and boulders deposited everywhere in the ice melt. What was it she always said? 'Landscape is living history.'

Kite came to a rock large enough to sit on, climbed up and stared into a deep pool of water. Tiny golden fish gathered in its mossy depths, glistening in the sun, like millions of coloured pixels. Then suddenly they were shoaling together, gathering into a shape she recognized as Dawn's face. The image of her friend was so accurate Kite felt she could reach out and touch her fine auburn hair as it floated under the water. Her face shone white and clear, and she smiled her gentle smile at Kite with her soft hazel eyes that reflected colours off the moss beneath her. Kite held her breath. Her heart raced with pure joy to see Dawn again so close. This must be what Dawn wanted too, to find a way of explaining what had happened. She reached out to her, down into the water, and the hundreds of tiny fish scattered in every direction, making her stumble backwards as a long shadow fell across the empty pool.

'We'd better get back to Boss-Nav if we're to arrive before dark!'

As Seth held out his hand to help her back on to the bank, the ground spun under her so that she felt as if she was about to pass out.

'Steady!' Seth grabbed her arm and pulled her to safety. 'You hardly touched your lunch. You've got to try to eat more,' he muttered as he walked her slowly back to the car.

Find Your Way

Now here they were, back at the stream, in the exact same place they'd been sitting half an hour before. There was no denying the fact that they'd been driving around in circles.

'Make a U-turn now!'

'That's back the way we just came. Some help you are!' Seth slammed his hand flat against the satnav. 'Have they not heard of street signs here?'

'There aren't any streets.'

A small flock of sheep approached the car, the one in front bleating loudly.

'OK, worth a try! Know the way to Mirror Falls?' Seth asked the vacant-looking ewe.

'Don't be an idiot!'

'At least this idiot can still make you laugh!'

Kite felt the muscles tense and her smile disappear as she forced herself to purse her lips closed. How could she laugh when Dawn was dead? The distorted sound of her own laughter echoed in her ears.

The ewe surveyed them with its docile black eyes, opened its mouth and appeared to yawn.

'Guess not! We should have asked that boy on the tractor.'

At the mention of him Kite felt the heat of embarrassment rise to her face.

'We could always turn around and head to that little pub we passed back there. They should know where it is.'

They heard it before they saw it. The sheep scattered in all directions at the first bark. A black sheepdog with a white flash came bounding towards them, ignoring the sheep and heading straight for Kite's open door. It laid its paws on her lap and flattened its head against her arm, panting contentedly.

'Where did *you* come from?' Kite stroked the dog's head.

Seth pointed further up the river to where a woman carrying a gnarled piece of driftwood for a walking stick slowly made her way towards them. Her coarse greying hair was pulled back into a severe ponytail, the taut strands drawn so tight over her ears that it made Kite's own scalp sting. She was wearing walking boots, trousers, a cheesecloth blouse and a waistcoat. In her right hand she carried a heavy-looking hessian sack. As she came closer Seth raised his hand in a friendly greeting and called out to her. Her blank expression did not change for a moment.

'Come away!' Her dog obediently leaped back from the car and returned to her side. Instead of moving closer, she stood stock still, so that Seth had to project his voice to be heard.

'We're looking for Mirror Falls,' he called over to her.

Still she did not approach.

'Take the track to where the land rises up there.' The woman pointed to a narrow path they had ruled out as hardly being wide enough for the car. 'There's a steep climb after that. Follow the track to the end – you can't miss it.' Her voice was clipped and sharp and carried across the land. Then unexpectedly she added, 'I'm going that way. I can show you if you want.' Her voice was still expressionless as she finally came towards them. 'As long as you don't mind Bardsey here.' The dog's ears pricked up at the sound of his name.

'Seems like a friendly soul!' Seth smiled, patting the dog's head as it offered him his paw.

'Down, Bardsey!' she ordered. 'He's still a puppy. I'm training him!' Her mouth betrayed a glimmer of a smile for the first time as Bardsey obediently returned to her side. Her arms rested firmly on her stick as she took the last steps towards the car and looked inside. She was not as old as Kite had first thought. Maybe Grandma Grace's age, in her sixties. Her skin was clear and unlined, not a face that had been exposed to the weather all its life. Only her blue-grey eyes seemed to fit with the mountain slate. She stared at Kite, and as she did her tight, closed expression shifted and a look of terrible sadness came over her. As she looked back into the woman's eyes Kite had the strangest sensation that this woman could see into her and was reading what was happening inside her. Then, dropping her driftwood stick and placing her hand on Kite's arm, she said the oddest thing: 'I'm sorry. I won't intrude. I hope you find your way.' She turned and strode powerfully away carrying her hessian sack and forgetting her walking stick altogether.

'There's plenty of room, really,' Seth called to her, but she ignored him and carried on her way. Kite wondered why she needed the stick at all.

'Come away, Bardsey!' she instructed in a firmer voice than before, and the dog picked up her stick, ran over and offered it to her before falling back in line at her heels.

Seth shrugged. 'Something I said?'

Kite lay down on the back seat and closed her eyes. Her mind was full of dreams and what could she call them . . . visions? Hallucinations? Dawn's grave, the Angel of the North, Dawn's reeds floating in the water, the giant carrying Dawn to safety, Dawn's face in the rock pool, the farm boy and now this crazy old woman. Kite raised her hand to her neck and held on to her St Christopher. She would have to get a hold of herself if she wasn't to go mad. She took a deep breath. She would be better when she'd slept more.

'Come on; don't give up on us now!' Seth urged the labouring car up the impossibly narrow track. 'Let's hope it doesn't rain, or this will turn into a river!'

As they passed the woman and her dog, she peered into the car. Something in the hessian sack she was carrying shifted. Whatever it was, it was the size of a large cat.

Kite shivered and rubbed her fingers over her St Christopher. Maybe her sleep-deprived mind was playing tricks on her, conjuring up all these strange images in its attempt to make sense of what had happened to Dawn. For the first time in her life she wished that she believed in something. She wished that Ruby had forced her to accompany her to church every week to sing in the choir and pray. Maybe if Kite could believe that Dawn had gone to a better place, then she would find a way to accept what Dawn had done, forgive her even. She would love to believe that Dawn's spirit was now set free into a peaceful haven, beautiful beyond human understanding. But the vision of Dawn's pitiful grave kept returning to her. Out of all the feelings she had about Dawn, it was the guilt that she hadn't been able to help her best friend that was eating her up, feeding off her so that she felt all shrivelled up inside.

Mirror Falls

'Come on! You can make it!' urged Seth as their car spluttered up the hill. 'Good job we're all stocked up on food! I would have liked to see the place in the light though,' he complained as they bumped along the final stretch of track. The light was fading fast as the courtyard and Mirror Falls came into view. The place was bathed in an eerie pink light, making the surrounding trees and the outline of the single-storey glass building resemble an etching. It appeared to Kite like an enormous glass barge jutting off the landscape, or perhaps a giant icicle.

'I'm feeling the pressure now,' gasped Seth. 'Sid's obviously expecting me to produce something completely original, sending me here!'

The sound of the waterfall was deafening. Kite vaguely remembered Seth saying something about it being directly under the building, but she'd had no idea what to expect. She opened the car window all the way down to let in the thunderous noise that seemed powerful enough to block out her thoughts. She felt as if she had entered some sort of parallel reality.

'I'll get out here!' she announced.

'I knew you'd be excited,' Seth called after her, as he drove off the dirt path and pulled into the sloping courtyard. It was made of large sandstone slabs, flattening out at the entrance – an imposing-looking sliding glass door. To its left was a giant earthenware pot containing a Japanese tree with spindly acid-green arms. Kite pressed her face against the cold glass and peered inside. There was a clear view from the entrance into the whole house. Through the kitchen she could see a wide corridor that opened out on to another huge room, with a spiral staircase to one side. Beyond that the room expanded further, ending in another mammoth window that mirrored the entrance. So they had come to an open-plan, see-through house! Unsettled, Kite began to wish that they were staying somewhere more normal, like the stone cottages with little protected windows and wild-flower gardens they'd passed on the way.

'The key is under the loose brick next to the acer!' Seth read the instructions out loud and wandered over to the huge pot. 'I wouldn't have thought this plant was indigenous to the area!' he commented as he lifted the brick and took out an electronic key. 'Mind you, neither is this house! Open sesame!' he laughed as he swiped the key-card across a metal sensor panel.

Not for the first time, Kite felt like running away from Seth.

'I'm just going to see the waterfall.' She walked back out into the courtyard.

'Don't be long,' Seth called after her.

She discovered a narrow path that fell away steeply below her. From somewhere under the building a great jet of water spurted out of a hole in the rock and dropped away into a chasm below. Kite walked on a few paces and froze. On a jagged ledge, just beyond reaching distance, lay the skeleton of a sheep; its hollow head twisted upward as if pleading for help. Water cascaded through its eye cavities. Is this what would happen to Dawn's body? Kite shuddered at the thought of the locket she'd given Dawn hanging off her bones. She caught her breath, felt the acid rise from her empty stomach and vomited bitter yellow mucus that seemed to tear at her guts as they contracted and she retched and retched until nothing was left inside her. Her legs were shaking as she scrambled back up the steep path towards the entrance.

'Are you going to help me unpack?' Seth called.

'I want to go home!' Kite said, shaking her head.

Seth gnawed on his lower lip as if giving himself time to search for an appropriate response. 'I'm exhausted, Kite. I've driven all this way. I think you are too,' he said, reaching for her face.

Kite stepped away from him so that he wouldn't smell the sick on her breath. All she needed now was a new bout of his fretting.

'Look how pale you are. I tell you what – let's sleep on it and see how you feel in the morning.'

'There's a dead sheep in the waterfall.' She felt icy cold again, just as she had on the Falling Day, standing outside Mr Scott's office. 'Frozen to the bone' – people said that, didn't they? That's how that poor sheep must have felt too when it fell off the path and realized it was stranded. She wondered how long it would have taken for it to give up bleating for help.

'Nature can be brutal. That must have been horrible for you. I'll move it first thing in the morning. But apart from that, what do you think?' Seth spread his arms out to show off the building. 'I've never stayed anywhere as plush as this. Come on, Kite, give it a chance, eh?' He took her by the shoulders and guided her through the entrance to the kitchen.

'Dresser . . . wood-burning stove . . . magnificent wooden table!' Seth enthused, running his hands over the smooth light wood. 'This will do!'

He had in his hands an instruction folder that he read from as he walked over to a dresser to the right of the stove and took out what looked like a TV remote.

'Says that this is the key to making things work around here.' He placed the folder on the table and took his reading glasses from his pocket.

Kite walked out of the kitchen and along a wide adjoining walkway with a plain white wall to its left and a glass wall to its right that formed the outside of the house. It was like a sort of bridge between two rooms. Under Kite's feet the floor was made of intermittent sandstone and glass panels, reminding her of stepping stones in a stream she'd crossed once with Dawn on a school trip to Wales. Dawn had picked her way cautiously across and Kite had leaped from stepping stone to stone, finally landing flat on her face and getting soaked. Dawn's Tinkerbell giggle echoed back at her. Under the panels of glass gushed the waterfall that seemed to mirror light backwards and forward off the building. She supposed that's why it was called Mirror Falls. The name was fitting, Kite thought as she glanced around the glass building; the mirror that Dawn and Kite had so often been reflected in together had fallen, shattered into a million pieces.

Kite peered down through the glass stepping stones, and on the third panel she took a step backwards on to the firm stone. Under this transparent panel, one step away from her, the sheep carcass was clearly visible. She stared at the water rushing through the skeleton. With or without the grim carcass there would never be anything peaceful about this place because it would always be moving beneath her feet.

'Don't dwell on that now!' Seth pleaded, taking her hand and dragging her through towards the living room. At the end of the indoor stepping-stone bridge, to her left there was a glass spiral staircase winding upward to a level above the glass ceiling of the living room. She was relieved to find that there was a loft-type upper floor to the house after all. Maybe the bedrooms would feel less exposed.

'Close your eyes!' Seth ordered, pulling her into a vast glass box of a living room with views on all sides, down through the floor and up to the sky.

They walked slowly towards the enormous window that seemed to frame the countryside. Kite followed the path of the waterfall through the steep-sided valley as it merged with the stream and meandered away into the distance. Surrounding the widening stream were green fields dotted with sheep and fell ponies. On one side was hard grey rock and on the other a long stretch of woodland. Kite winced as the sky produced a perfect palette of pale pink and orange to replace the bright blues of the day. It was as if a master painter was at work. She felt as if she had been picked up from Dawn's graveside and dropped into this picture-perfect world, except that everything about it felt fake to her, like a cover-up. Apart from the grim sheep's carcass; *that* felt real enough.

As Kite stared down at the gaping drop beneath she wondered if it was possible for her to have drifted into a worse place. If she'd been asked to draw a building that looked how she felt at this moment, she would have drawn Mirror Falls. How was it possible for so much of the building to be hanging off the mountain without it careering into the chasm below? One thing was for certain. Whoever had dreamed up this house wanted to turn things on their head, to challenge nature.

'And – if that doesn't impress you – you'd better prepare yourself for this!' Seth indicated the dark purple sofa behind her. 'Sitting comfortably?' He pressed down on the large cushions to test them.

Kite nodded.

'Then I'll begin!'

A smooth whirring noise came from somewhere above her head, and she noticed that Seth was pointing the remote upward. As she watched, the huge glass sheet panel retracted, leaving nothing above but the open sky.

Kite picked up a cream woollen throw that was folded on the back of the sofa and wrapped it around her shoulders. 'Impressive!' Her voice was as expressionless as that of the strange woman they'd met on the road. 'But could you close it for now? I feel cold.'

Seth pressed the button and the roof slid back over them again. 'Why don't you go up and choose your bedroom, and I'll fix us something to eat?' he suggested. 'I'll bring your case up when I've unpacked the car.'

Kite walked around the sofa towards the stepping-stone bridge and began to climb the glass staircase. The banister was carved from driftwood like the old woman's walking stick. She ran her fingers along its winding surface. The unevenness of the wood with its random knots was comforting after the unforgiving harsh lines of the house. At the top was a narrow glass corridor with three misted-glass doorways leading off it. The wall at the end overlooked the living area and valley below. She looked down through the landing to the stepping-stone bridge and beyond that, through one of the glass panels, to the waterfall. There it was again: the macabre reminder of death. From here she could just see its skull.

Kite walked along the corridor to the third door, slid it open and peered inside. She was relieved to find that the bedroom had a sturdy sandstone floor covered by a thick woollen rug. The tiny room contained nothing but a low wooden bed with plain white linen, a coarse cream homespun blanket, a bedside table and an enormous floor-to-ceiling bookshelf. She scanned the colourful spines. There would be no shortage of reading material, if she decided to hole herself up here for the summer. If Dawn was here she would work her way through book after book. Kite reached up and touched one of the heavy old tomes, and another remote fell off the shelf. She pressed a button, and the whole wall of books opened on to a wardrobe with shelves, drawers, hangers and places to store shoes, even a desk and a lamp. Kite smiled, despite herself.

But the thing she liked best about the room was the two sturdy walls painted in stone and heather purple. She could see now that the little colour that was scattered around the house was inspired by the surrounding landscape. The fourth wall, at the far end of the room, was misted glass, with a large clear circular window inset. Kite walked over to the spyhole and peered out. Then she stepped three paces back and lay on the bed, her head propped up on the downy pillows. From here she had a perfect view of the valley. She felt like a bird nesting high up in the trees and surveying the mountainside for possible dangers. If she *had* to stay here, at least she'd found somewhere in this strange, unbalanced house where she could hide away.

Seth sang to himself contentedly as he unpacked the car, trailing in and out with bags and food. She knew it was mean-spirited of her, but Kite wished he would attempt to curb his enthusiasm for the trip for just one moment. It was like he was trying, by the sheer force of his happy nature, to push her uphill to a better place. But as she listened to him singing she resolved to try to be less snappy. She could see how hard he'd tried, despite everything, to rescue her birthday – even though it had been the longest, most arduous day of her life.

'Are you coming down?' Seth called from the bottom of the staircase. 'I've made hot chocolate.'

'Coming!' Kite called back, standing up and noticing a painted door in the stone-coloured wall. She pushed it and found herself in a luxurious ultra-modern bathroom, all mirrors and clean white surfaces, with a double sink, a shower in the corner and a huge bath sunken into the middle of the floor. She walked over to the sink and washed the smell of vomit from her hands and face. Now she had seen her room, she wanted to unpack her things, hang her clothes up and find a safe place in the secret wardrobe for Dawn's precious things.

Kite looked over at the deep sunken bath and longed to fill it with hot water and wash herself in Dawn's soap. A tube of unopened toothpaste sat on a shelf. She smeared some on her finger and over her teeth and rinsed. As she dried her hands and face she walked through a door on the opposite side of the bathroom that led to another bedroom. Here there was no amazing bookshelf and no view either, just a simple sliding wardrobe and a peephole on to the corridor . . .

'Did you get the best room then?' Seth asked as she walked down the stairs.

'Of course!'

On a little table to the side of the sofa, Seth had placed a couple of mugs of hot chocolate and two slices of Ruby's birthday cake. He handed Kite a plate and she began to eat, just to please him. The milky chocolate soothed her empty stomach, warming her from the inside.

'Let's call Ruby.' Seth picked up his mobile, pressed her number then looked a bit puzzled as he walked around the room.

'There was no mention of this in their booklet! No television OK, but the no-computer, no-signal thing just doesn't make sense in a house like this! There's not even a DVD player. I wish I'd brought my laptop now; at least we could have watched a few films! I've been wondering why Sid said he'd got it surprisingly cheaply from the agency! Rubes will go mad,' he groaned, discarding his phone on the sofa. 'Well, it looks like it's just you and me, kid!' he joked, putting on his awful American accent.

'Funny!'

'Don't worry, we'll find somewhere to call her from tomorrow. Anyway, she'll be here before you know it.' Seth yawned. 'You be all right if I go and have a lie-down? I'll get up and make us supper later. That drive didn't half do me in.'

Kite nodded.

'If the noise of the waterfall gets too much for you, we can apparently play God and switch nature on and off at the touch of a button! Here, have a play!' Seth handed Kite the remote, patted the back of her hair and climbed the staircase.

She heard him exclaiming with delight as he explored upstairs.

'Yep! You've definitely got the best room!' he shouted down.

Kite flicked a switch and the house grew eerily quiet. She turned the remote over in her hands. How did it do that? If only it really was this easy to control nature, to walk over to the stepping-stone bridge, flick a switch and make that sheep carcass reconstruct itself; to start growing a heart and lungs, sinews and muscles; to fuse its bones. She would fill it with blood travelling through its veins and make it grow a woolly coat to be warm again, and she wouldn't stop until it began to bleat at the top of its voice.

Blind

Metal clanked at the front of the house and a dog barked, making Kite jump bolt upright. She wondered if Seth had heard the noise too and she thought about calling for him, but his stuttery snore was already echoing through the house. Cautiously she walked over the bridge, stepping over the glass panels and sticking to the sturdier stone. She pressed a button on the wall beside the entrance and the glass slid open. There was no one there, but a folded note lay on the sandstone walkway, peeping from underneath the Japanese tree.

Kite stepped out, picked up the envelope and walked briskly back inside, pressing the button behind her. The door closed and made a little click-locked noise that helped her feel a little more secure. As she walked over the bridge she caught flashes of the sheepdog as he ran along the path below. The woman was feeling her way down the uneven track by the side of the waterfall, steadying herself from time to time with her driftwood stick. In her other hand she was holding a torch. Bardsey looked up and barked a friendly greeting at Kite. She waved but the woman did not wave back. Instead she nodded twice, raised her stick in the air and wandered on with her empty hessian sack draped over her shoulders like a shawl. What had she done with its contents?

Kite followed the path of the woman and her dog along the stream and through the darkening valley. Then, as she realized that she herself was sitting in the gloom she stood up and searched along the walls for the light switch. She couldn't find one, so she picked up the remote control and pressed a button at random. A huge blind, lit from above, unravelled from a wall cavity. On the back someone had painted an abstract impression of the landscape. Kite flicked another button and the blind lifted again. She could still see the flickering torchlight in the distance.

Kite looked down at the letter. She supposed she should wait till Seth woke up to open it but . . .

The address at the top of the quality paper that read 'Mirror Falls, Swindale, Cumbria' had been scored out, as had all the letters after the name . . . Agnes Landseer. So that woman had once lived here. For all Kite knew, she even owned the house. Kite read on.

Underneath was written '*Scar View*' and the words.

'*For everyone's sake. All I ask is that you lower the blind every night.*'

What? How weird was that? The woman must be mad. Her name suited her. Agnes was old fashioned, sharp and matter of fact, and Landseer made Kite think of something slightly spooky, someone who could see things on the land, ghosts or spirits maybe. Kite shivered as she remembered the way Agnes had seemed to look into her and then refused to get in the car.

Kite walked back over to the window. Agnes's torch beam remained steady. Was she watching the house? Perhaps when Kite had inadvertently lowered the blind, Agnes had thought that she was doing what she was told. Kite felt the anger rise up in her again. Why should she be dictated to by a stranger? And what was the point of having a house made of glass if you couldn't watch the sun set and the moon rise? Kite lay down and watched the multitude of stars reflecting off the glass. Where was Dawn now in this vast glistening universe? Had she appeared to her in the stream because she was somewhere nearby?

If only she could take herself back to Fairview, run down to Dawn's flat on the night before it happened. And instead of Facebooking, *talk* to her and make her see that things were not as bad as she'd thought. If she could have caught her right there at her low point, then Dawn might be sitting in her room now, practising for her next concert. Or she might even have come up here to the Lakes with them. She could imagine her listening to the waterfall, picking up her oboe and playing a piece of watery music. Kite took Dawn's iPod out of her pocket, plugged in her earphones and let the music float over her. As she stared at the moon, a tiny wisp of a cloud floated over its surface and her mind cleared. It all made sense now: her dreams in the car, Dawn's face in the rock pool, even the sheep's carcass; they were all signs. Dawn was coming to talk to *her*, to answer her questions, to take away all the aching pain, guilt, bitterness, anger and terrible sadness. Dawn *wants* me to be close to her, Kite told herself.

Imprint

A high-pitched screech cut through the rare peace of Kite's sleep. She sprang bolt upright on the sofa, her heart thudding so loud it almost drowned out the sound of the waterfall. And then she saw it, with its wings stretched to their widest expanse, every cream feather dappled with brown, lit from behind by the moon, like an X-ray image. As it glided towards her beyond the glass, the owl lifted its heart-shaped face upward to reveal Dawn's delicate features and her iridescent moon pallor . . . then it SMASHED itself into the glass, with the speed and violence of gunshot. For a second it seemed that it hung there, stunned; then it dropped away. Kite stared down through the gloom as the feathered form spiralled out of control towards the gully.

Perhaps the screech had been hers after all, because Seth came hurtling down the stairs, shouting at the top of his voice.

'What on earth's wrong?'

Kite folded her legs under herself and hugged her knees tight in a fetal position, rocking backwards and forward. Seth placed an arm around her shoulders and held her close as she whimpered in fear.

'What is it?' persisted Seth, looking around to see what could possibly have traumatized her.

Kite lifted her right arm and pointed towards the great expanse of window.

'There's nothing there!' Seth picked up the remote control and switched on the dimmer lights. Now he stepped closer. Etched on the glass was the perfect imprint of an owl.

'Poor thing!' Seth traced his fingers over the outline. 'Hopefully just stunned.' He looked down towards the ground below and then turned back to Kite.

'You know, that scream of yours was enough to wake the dead!'

Kite stared at him, her heart still thudding violently in her chest.

'Sorry! I didn't mean . . .' Seth trailed off.

'It's OK, I'm OK,' Kite reassured him. 'It was just the shock of it!'

What she couldn't tell him was that for the first time since the Falling Day she felt something like hope stirring inside her, even if it was mixed up with fear of the unknown. She had wished for Dawn to come and find her, and as soon as the owl had flown towards her she'd felt in her gut that Dawn was back.

Owl Feather

It didn't matter that she hadn't slept or that her mind had raced all night as she listened to Dawn's music. When she unwrapped the lemon soap the next morning she felt as if she could breathe again. It was the most luxurious bath that she had ever had. The tub had jacuzzi bubbles and a pillow for her head, but the best thing about it was that when she got out she smelt Dawn all around her.

'Breakfast!' Seth shouted up from the kitchen, his voice competing with the cascading echo of the waterfall.

'Coming!' Kite called back as she dried herself, rummaging in her bag and throwing on some leggings and a T-shirt.

Downstairs she was relieved to find the Dawn owl still stretched across the living-room window. There was the proof. Kite cast her eyes down through the valley to see where Agnes could have been heading the night before. Right at the end of the

132

valley was a raised egg-like mound of rocks.

'What is another word for "Basket of egg scenery?"' The question from her Geography exam came back to her.

'Try revising! Roche Moutonnée, idiot!' Kite laughed out loud at the sound of Dawn's voice so clear and close to her.

'Now that's something I haven't heard for a while!' Seth drew her into a hug. 'That giggle of yours.'

'Nor me!' Kite smiled, as Dawn's voice still echoed through her head. She looked down through the glass panels to the empty ledge.

'Did you move the sheep?'

'No – probably got washed away.' Seth shrugged and wandered away to finish making breakfast. 'How was your bath? Can't wait to have a wallow in there myself!'

'Good.'

Kite sat at the beechwood table. In front of her, propped up between jam pots, was the weird note about the blinds. She picked it up and read it again.

'I read that just now!' Seth said, placing a mug of tea in front of her.

'Last night when you were asleep, that woman with the dog came by. She didn't knock or anything, just left the note outside!' Kite took a sip of sweet tea.

'When we go to the village later, I intend to find

out about her. Something's not quite right there.' Seth tapped his nose and narrowed his eyes in a mock Sherlock Holmes gesture.

'You don't need to be cheerful around me all the time. I know you're not. I saw you crying in the car yesterday.' Kite was surprised by the sharpness of her own words, and as soon as they escaped her mouth she felt sorry. This was exactly how she had decided not to be.

Seth paused with his back to her as he buttered the toast, then turned to Kite and handed her the plate.

'There's no shame in crying. You know, it's lovely to hear you laughing again, but it might help if you could cry too.'

'It's hard to cry when everyone's telling you to,' Kite answered.

'I know.' Seth sighed and sat down at the table opposite her. 'Spoke to Rubes this morning. I only had to walk to the end of the track. You should have heard the mouthful she gave me for not calling last night! She sends her love though. She asked how you are. I said I thought you were a bit better. You slept well last night, didn't you?'

'Yep!' Kite lied as she stood up to avoid his searching gaze and padded barefoot out into the sunshine of the courtyard, chewing on the corner of her toast.

The very last thing she expected to find was another note under the Japanese tree, exactly where the first had been. As she bent down to pick it up one of the branches bowed and a delicate leaf brushed her cheek. She felt as if Dawn was a mere breath away from her. She walked further into the courtyard. Her hands shook as she opened the note. There were the same crossings out and the name Agnes Landseer and the new address of '*Scar View.*'

Perhaps you'll take notice NOW! PLEASE close the blinds at night, for the sake of the owls.

Kite looked back through the building at the ghostly shape of the Dawn owl pinned against the glass. As she read the note over again she wondered what that strange woman, who had once lived in this house, knew about the owls? She felt her cheek where the soft branch of the Japanese tree had reached out to her like a human hand of friendship. She would do what Agnes Landseer ordered, for Dawn's sake.

'So this is what they call a cantilever house!' Seth mused as they stood under the building. 'I was reading that they have to put enough weight on one end so that the rest will have the confidence to jut out into space without falling flat on its face!

'I wonder how long the owl print will stay?' he continued, as they scrambled down under Mirror Falls in search of the fallen owl. With the sun glinting off the glass, the imprint was less visible from this angle. 'The windows are supposed to be self-cleaning, impossible to get a ladder to them –' Seth surveyed the steep angle up to the living-room window – 'but I think it'll take some rain to wash that away.'

Maybe, thought Kite it will only fade when Dawn has given me the answers to all my questions. She looked up at the cloudless sky. That didn't look like it would be any time soon. Anyway, she didn't want it to fade, not until she could make sense of why the Dawn owl was seeking her out.

'I suppose the poor thing could have been washed away, like the sheep.' Seth sighed.

'Wait!' Kite called after him, reaching out her hands as a falling creamy-white feather came wafting towards her. She caught it and clasped it in her hands as if she was holding on to her best friend. 'Dawn,' she whispered. Now she knew for sure that she was not imagining it. Here was another sign. As she let her fingers brush over the soft feathers she felt comforted by the presence of Dawn's spirit all around her.

'I think she was just stunned,' Kite said as she caught up with Seth. 'She must have flown away.'

Seth smiled at Kite and linked arms with her. 'How do you know it was a she-owl?' he asked as they began to climb the steep path home. Kite shrugged but there was no doubt in her mind.

'I just know!'

Carrec Arms

Driving through Swindale Common they passed a small group of boys around Kite's age jogging along the road. A tall boy wolf-whistled as he caught sight of Kite through the open window, and the others laughed.

'If you've got breath enough to whistle at the lasses, then you should be running faster!' the boy in front called back in a soft Lake District accent. It was the boy who had been driving the tractor. When he recognized the car he looked inside and smiled at Kite with his sparkling grey eyes.

'Do you know her?' the boy behind called to him in a thick Birmingham accent.

'Not yet!' she heard him reply as Seth negotiated his way over the cattle-grid.

'Do you think you might start running again, when you feel a bit stronger?' Seth asked.

Kite shrugged as she looked through the side

mirror at the farmer boy urging the others on into a sprint.

The Carrec Arms was a limewashed stone building positioned in the middle of a hamlet of tiny cottages. Inscribed on an ancient stone lintel above the pub's low doorway was the date (1606) in Roman numerals. Seth ducked and went through. Inside there was only a single room, with a bar at the far end. Even the colours of the place, bathed in soft amber light, seemed to soothe. There was nothing bright or dazzling or new here. The beams were dark oak, all gnarled and knotted. Copper and silver pennies had been wedged into the gaps between the beams. In one thick opening someone had lodged a line of £1 coins. Kite wondered how long these would have lasted in a London pub.

The windows were so tiny and deepset that hardly any light from the bright day outside filtered through. A small fire burned in a blackened grate at one end of the room despite the heat of the day. One long ancient oak table, benches on either side, dominated the room. The wood was smooth and indented where generations of bottoms must have worn down the surface. Two grand-looking chairs were placed at either end of the table, one housing an old man who was dozing. A vase of wild summer flowers sat in the middle. The room smelt of sweet cow parsley, burning wood, ale and herbs.

In the other chair a small, middle-aged Indian-looking man with a jovial round face and wavy black hair turned and smiled at Kite. It made her feel more at home that he looked so comfortably ensconced here. She had a hunch that he might feel pleased to see her too, and all of this odd logic seemed to be contained in the nod that passed between them.

'What can I get you?' a pretty blonde woman with rosy cheeks asked Seth, pulling herself away from a sink full of washing-up. She was wearing a worn old-fashioned apron dotted with flowers.

Seth ordered a beer, and a cider for Kite.

'Mind if we join you?' he asked the Indian man, who smiled in answer and held out his hand to shake as Seth and Kite nudged along the bench.

'Ajay Sherpa.' He offered Seth a firm handshake.

'My name's Ellie,' the woman from behind the bar called over.

Seth introduced himself and paused for a moment to see if Kite would follow his lead. But she stayed silent, and so he introduced her too. Seth had always been able to put people at their ease and slip into a conversation. In fact Kite and Seth were usually a bit of a double act. Since the Falling Day, though, Kite had become almost silent in company. And as soon as Kite discovered that Ajay Sherpa was the local doctor, she decided that she would not say a word. She could see it all panning out. The next thing, she knew, Seth would be trying to make an appointment for her.

As Seth chatted away Kite peered at the old man dozing at the head of the table. The lines on his face were deeply scored. Kite had never really looked at such an ancient face before. Compared to this man, Grandma Grace looked youthful, with her big swirl of grey hair and smooth, oiled skin. The old man's mouth drooped slightly and saliva trickled down his chin as he wheezed in his sleep.

'Jack used to run this pub. Ellie over there's his granddaughter,' explained Dr Sherpa. 'He pretty much brought her up. He'll be getting his letter from the Queen soon – not that he's waiting for that!' he joked in a soft sing-song mixture of Indian and Northern accents that Kite had never heard before.

Kite couldn't help staring at the old man. As he slept, he began to resemble the oak beams that surrounded him, she thought, as she tuned in and out of Dr Sherpa's stories of growing up in Nepal.

'No better place for a mountain goat like me,' he was saying now. 'You know, I can't believe it was twenty-five years ago that I came here. Nobody else wanted the job of travelling between the villages and farms in all weathers. So I moved here with my family and we converted our barn. You must come and eat with us!' Dr Sherpa turned to Kite, who was struggling to keep her eyes open. 'Sorry to say that we're a bit of an ageing population around here – apart from you summer visitors. I hope we don't bore you to death!'

Kite shook her head politely. There was the 'death' word again. How many births and deaths had Dr Sherpa attended? If it was an old population, it was probably more deaths than births. He seemed like such a contented person, she couldn't imagine that he had ever had to face something as traumatic as a young girl taking her own life. For the first time Kite thought about all the people who might have touched Dawn's body after she died, examining her, prodding her, dressing her, finding out the cause of death, the time of death. She had always been such a private person; it made Kite want to heave.

Ellie brought Dr Sherpa a fresh cup of tea and sat down on the opposite side of the bench. Kite looked up at Seth, who was still smiling and laughing. It must be a relief for him to be among this welcoming collection of strangers, away from her sadness and silence.

'I'll be happy to come and play a gig, if you'll have me!' he was saying to Ellie.

'Not exactly the O2, but you'd be surprised how many folk we can cram in! Once the younger folk get to hear of it, we get the campers and the kids from the outward-bound school up the road; some of them even come in from town on a Saturday night,' Ellie chatted on.

After a while Seth took Agnes Landseer's cryptic notes from his pocket. At the sight of them, Ellie and Dr Sherpa exchanged a knowing glance. According to the doctor, Agnes was a bit of a recluse, but Kite had the impression that he was holding back. She supposed he was not allowed to talk about his patients.

'You probably don't know this, but she's your landlady – even though the place is let through an agency. No one really understands what happened to Agnes. She fought so hard to get Mirror Falls built; you would have thought her life depended on it. It was supposed to be her dream home. She's a famous architect, got buildings all over Europe,' Dr Sherpa explained.

Kite tried to square the picture of the strange old woman they'd met on the road with this description.

'We're talking about Craggy Aggie, Grandad! She's been unsettling the visitors again – sending her addled notes,' Ellie shouted over to Jack. With his right hand he wiped his mouth, adjusted something in his ear and snorted, sending a spray of saliva across the table. Kite noticed that his left hand lay flat and lifeless by his side. She thought how strange it must feel to have only one side of yourself that you could control. Ellie let out a little embarrassed laugh, then gently wiped away his spittle with a cloth. Jack's old eyes opened again and settled on Seth, who shifted slightly on the bench.

'In the end, Grandad fought against that building

going up. He got that het up about it, we all think it was the cause of his stroke,' Ellie spoke this quietly, turning away from Jack, and then back to him, raising her voice once more. 'You're no great fan of Craggy Aggie, are you, Grandad? Shame you had to sell her the land in the first place.'

The old man banged his good hand on the table, as if ordering Ellie to stop talking. It was surprising how much strength was still held in his ancient body.

'Don't get yourself all worked up about it again. I suppose we'll never know now what went on.'

The old man nodded, closing his eyes tight.

Dr Sherpa poured tea into his saucer and took a great slurp. 'I don't know why, but somehow it always tastes better like this!' He smiled. 'We all have our odd ways. I suppose Agnes is to birds what I am to humans!' Dr Sherpa let out a hearty laugh as if he'd said something funny. 'She calls on me from time to time on her way to the vet's, and of course I go over there to check on her. It must be a lonely life,' he confided. 'Birds, her garden, her dog and her grandson are pretty much all she cares about. If you saw the way she looks out for the injured owls she picks up here and there, you'd know she means no harm.'

A vision of Agnes carrying her hessian sack entered Kite's mind. Maybe she'd been hunting around under Mirror Falls and picked up the Dawn owl too.

'We had an owl fly into our window last night. It

left a perfect print.' Seth said to Dr Sherpa, glancing tentatively at Kite as if he was afraid of upsetting her.

'Aggie explained to me once how they make their mark,' Dr Sherpa mused. 'Something about the oil and the powder on the feathers sticking to the glass like a fingerprint.'

'You know what they say when a great bird like that flies at you!' Ellie spread her plump arms out in a mock scary pose.

Seth stood up abruptly. 'I'll have another beer!' he interjected, walking over to the bar. Kite could tell by his hushed whisper that he was filling Ellie in on what had happened to Dawn.

'Of course it's all a lot of folklore and ghosting tales!' Ellie muttered as she returned to wipe the table.

'What *do* they say?' asked Kite.

'No, nothing. I told you, it's a lot of nonsense I was talking. I'm so sorry about your friend,' Ellie said softly. 'I lost my parents in an accident years ago, so sadness is no stranger at my door.'

Kite raised her hand to her scar and pulled her hair down over it. She wanted to stand up right now and run as far away from these people as it was possible to get. What business had Seth to tell these strangers about Dawn? They couldn't know anything about how she was feeling. Dr Sherpa shot a questioning look from Seth to Kite. She felt as if he was examining her.

'Can we go now?' Kite whispered.

'When we've been introduced.' Seth nodded towards Jack, who was staring at Seth as if he was trying to remember where he'd seen him before.

'Have you joined us, Jack? This is Seth and Kite,' said Dr Sherpa. 'Your hearing aid working all right now, Jack?' he asked, tapping his own ear.

A smile spread over Jack's face as he looked at Kite. He lifted his stick and pointed to a faded sepia photo among the gallery on the wall behind him. Ellie reached up, took the photo off the wall and placed it in Jack's hands. The image was of a group of mud-smeared young men in long shorts, with bare feet and chests, rain lashing their faces. One of them, running ahead of the others, was flying a kite.

'Grandad was a fell runner in his time. "King of the Fells" they named him. The winner always gets to fly the Carrec kite – isn't that so, Grandad?'

Kite stared into the image and back to Jack, whose smile was still recognizable. She thought she could trace something in the fine paper-thin lines of his face that was still, after all this time, strong and full of energy.

Jack swallowed hard as if he was desperate to speak.

'Kite's a keen runner too.'

'Not really!' Kite mumbled. She wished Seth would stop trying to draw her into the conversation. Now the doctor was definitely shooting her inquisitive glances.

'No doubt Grandad would have given you a run for your money!' Ellie joked, but the old man had pushed the photo aside now.

'Seth's been telling me his mam's family were from around here,' Dr Sherpa said loudly and clearly.

Suddenly Jack propped himself up in his chair, his back bolt upright, holding his right hand in the air like a claw and twisting it this way and that.

'That's a question,' explained Dr Sherpa.

Jack patted his chest.

'Now you've got him following a scent!' Ellie said. 'Grandad's helped folk who've turned up from all over the spot coming here to find their roots. I always said he should have written a book.'

Jack tapped Ellie's hand.

'What was your mam's name?'

'Jackson,' Seth answered automatically.

The old man scrunched his brow and shook his head from side to side.

'Sorry, I mean Storey . . . my mum's name was Storey. She grew up in a children's home in Sheffield, but I think her parents came from around here.'

On hearing the name Storey, the old man shuffled back in his chair and attempted to stand. Dr Sherpa walked around the table to help him and Jack placed an arm over his shoulder. Then he took a step towards Seth and held out his hand. Seth shook it gently. People are meant to grow old, thought Kite, staring at Jack's hands; a map of blue veins and jutting bones. How many concerts would Dawn have played if she'd lived until she was as old as Jack?

'Storey's a local name all right,' said Ellie. 'If he or any of his friends knows anything, he'll find a way of telling you. Even though he can't write or talk, he makes himself understood. The photos help.'

Seth nodded and walked over to the gallery. Here was Jack, standing in a boat with a fly-fishing rod, proudly holding up his catch; a gathering of men, sleeves rolled up, a pile of sheep fleeces in front of them as they each raised a glass to the camera; a waterfall; a smiling, moustached Jack wearing khaki uniform, his arms wrapped around a pretty girl; a whole series of pictures charting the building of an enormous wall.

'Those are of the construction of the Haweswater Dam,' she explained. 'Somewhere under all that water is the farm where Grandad grew up. Lots of these families around here did. Maybe yours too,' Ellie told Seth. 'You should take a walk down there, see what you make of it. Folk are saying the last time it dried right out like this was a good twenty-five years back.'

Kite's attention was caught by a row of tiny black-and-white photographs of Indian women carrying pots on their heads; a turbaned man having a shave on a street pavement; a naked bald man holding his copper begging bowl; and a sleeping brown-eared dog under the shade of a tree. Dr Sherpa followed Kite's gaze.

'These are from Jack's service in India. He shared so many stories of his time there with me, before he lost his speech. You should look after these, Ellie; they must be quite a rare collection.'

Kite felt that she had been wrong to assume that these people belonged to an inward-looking world. Whatever was happening to her, she knew one thing for sure – that she had come here to learn. Perhaps it was the place and its people that had drawn Dawn's spirit here too.

At a certain point the photographs moved into colour, but even these seemed to be faded now. There were pictures of Jack proudly holding a baby; of children running wild on the fells carrying baskets full of giant mushrooms and sitting on walls like gatherings of birds waiting to fly. Jack raised his arm and ran his hand along the row of children as if he was trying to remember who was who. He bashed the side of his head in frustration.

'If only he could write things down, but his good hand is so riddled with arthritis he can't hold a pen,' explained Ellie, taking the photo off the wall and laying it on the table.

Jack shook his head as if he was lost somewhere in the past. That's how it was supposed to be, thought Kite; you should get so old that you can look back across time and only vaguely remember what happened in different parts of your life. As far as she knew, the last photo of the two of them together was taken on Dawn's birthday. Kite wondered if Hazel and Jimmy would be able to bring themselves to line the walls of their new flat with all those captured moments of Dawn's life. For her part Kite couldn't stand to look at any photos of the two of them now. She'd brought none with her.

'*Please*, can we go?' Kite whispered to Seth.

'Don't you worry!' Ellie reassured Seth as they were leaving. 'If your grandma lived around here, Grandad's sure to have some information for you.'

Jack patted Seth's hand and his mouth stretched into the widest of smiles, revealing a motley collection of higgledy-piggledy teeth that were hanging on for dear life.

'Kite!' Ellie called after her. Seth was watching and she felt that it would be rude to ignore her, so she walked reluctantly over to the bar. 'You know if you need to talk to someone, it was Dr Sherpa who helped me more than anyone else when my parents died.'

'Thank you,' said Kite uncomfortably, and headed for the door.

'I'd better be going too, as Jack seems in fine fettle today,' Dr Sherpa scraped back his chair. 'So I'll pop in to see you at Mirror Falls.'

Seth nodded pointedly as if he'd made a definite appointment.

It was as she'd feared. Thanks to Seth, they all knew – and they were all going to try to help.

Owl Lore

On the way home Kite had to listen to Seth moaning on about how frustrating it was that he couldn't get an Internet connection to do more research.

'I'll have to drive to a library and maybe even a town hall tomorrow to look things up in the book of births, deaths and marriages.'

'Good! Then maybe it'll stop you blabbing about Dawn to everyone.'

He looked hurt, and once again she immediately felt sorry for being so vicious. Seth drove along in silence, then switched on the radio; a dance beat throbbed out – the sort of thing that Kite usually loved and Seth hated. Instead of switching channel he glanced over at Kite and tapped on the steering wheel as if he was enjoying it. A few months ago she would have cranked the track up as loud as possible. It was the kind of beat that once it got under your skin could take you over, but now it did the opposite, jarring her nerves and making her head pound with tiredness.

Kite hit the radio button with a flat hand to silence the low insistent beat, then plugged herself into Dawn's iPod. Listening to recordings of Dawn's playing felt a bit like reading a book where Dawn had made notes in the margins or folded over the corner of a page, like witnessing Dawn's thoughts and emotions in action. She turned up the volume and let the deep, familiar music calm her.

Seth stared at the road ahead, his mouth tightly closed. After a while he pulled over on to a verge. Kite turned the volume down to hear him talking to Ruby, telling her how beautiful the countryside was, how warm and welcoming people were here, and about the soft lilt of their voices, and the vivid turn of phrase that he wanted to capture in his ballads. He spoke about Jack and then Mirror Falls and how much she would love it when she visited. He said how being here had sparked a new urgency to find out about his family. It was what he didn't talk about by the time he passed her the phone that interested Kite.

'Haven't heard him this fired up to write in years!' Ruby said. 'And how about you, my darlin'. What do you think of the place?'

Kite didn't know how to reply. What she did know for sure was that if she told Ruby or Seth or Dr Sherpa that she felt Dawn was trying to reach her here, they would probably worry about her even more. But somewhere deep inside her she knew that

151

she had been drawn here for a purpose as strongly as Seth had, and now she had no choice but to stay.

'Kite? Are you all right, my darlin'?'

'Fine.'

'And Seth said you slept all the way up to the Lakes. How have you been sleeping since you got there?'

'Much better.'

She hadn't slept more than a few moments at a time, but she knew if she told Ruby the truth she would probably jump on the next train up here. Who knows, maybe Dr Sherpa would have her admitted to hospital like she'd overheard Seth and Ruby talking about in London, and she couldn't risk that because it would mean missing out on whatever it was that Dawn was trying to tell her.

When Ruby and Kite had said their goodbyes, Seth took the phone off her, opened the door and walked away from the car. He paced along the boundary of a dry stone wall, picking bits of moss from between the crevices. Even though she was too far away to hear what he was saying, his pacing up and down made Kite feel uncomfortable. He was listening to Ruby more than he was speaking and that made her nervous. What new thing did Ruby think would be good for her now? Seth kicked shards of slate aside as he listened – now he seemed to be arguing with Ruby. As he ambled back towards the car Kite cranked up the volume on her iPod and pretended to be fast asleep. Seth placed a little posy of heather that he'd collected on her knee.

'Yeah, it's lovely blue skies and wall-to-wall sun so far – the locals are saying it's unheard of!' he told Ruby cheerily . . . as if they'd been talking about the weather all this time.

'I don't care what they say about that woman Agnes, she's created something exquisite in this house,' declared Seth as they walked back into Mirror Falls. He pressed the remote to slide back the living-room roof, then sauntered over to the window. If anything, the owl print showed up even clearer against the backdrop of the deepening fiery sky.

'We'd better close the blinds then, if it's landlady's orders! We don't want any more birds injured. I suppose they must get disorientated if they can't tell the glass is there.' He pressed the button for the blinds. 'Shame to miss the sunset, but that's pretty good too,' Seth whistled as the enormous abstract painting of the valley unfolded.

As they lay at opposite ends of the sofa, Kite began to ponder about Agnes Landseer. Why would you design and build a place as extraordinary as this as your retirement home, and then leave it? And why did Jack seem so disturbed by even the mention of Agnes's name?

Seth began his familiar light wheezy snore. She

covered him with a throw and walked up the spiral staircase and into the bathroom. She filled the sink and reached into the cupboard where she had hidden Dawn's soap. She let the rich lemony scent seep into her skin. It was uncanny how that smell could summon Dawn into the room. Kite placed the soap on the side and walked into her bedroom, pressing the remote to open the bookshelf, behind which she had created a den out of cushions and blankets, like the ones she and Dawn used to make in primary school. She snuggled under the woollen blanket and took out Dawn's reed box. With great care she flicked up the little copper catch and prised the lid open. There was Dawn's golden reed. She eased it out, holding it between her thumb and index finger and raised it to her mouth. Then she took a sharp breath in and blew as hard as she could, but no sound emerged. Kite placed the reed back in the box and hid it under her den pillows with her Dawn feather and her unopened birthday card.

It was snug in here, and being so close to Dawn's precious things might help her sleep. Maybe Dawn would come to her in her dreams.

'Close your eyes and open your senses, my darlin'.' She heard Ruby's soothing voice like a lullaby in her head.

Rush of waterfall . . . click of switch in the kitchen below . . . something electrical turning itself off.

154

Sheep bleating . . . dog barking, or perhaps too high-pitched for a dog. Maybe foxes mating in the dark then . . . And yes, there it was, hollow and clear, the insistent hoot of an owl. What was Dawn trying to tell her? There was no way that she could sleep. The cacophony of her own mind was even louder than the waterfall. She threw off the blanket, crawled out of her den and surveyed the bookshelf. Her attention was caught by a thick coffee-table tome on the top shelf. Its cover was stained and the pages well thumbed. *Owl Lore*. The title was written in old-fashioned swirly writing and a giant owl face stared from the cover. She shivered. This could not be a coincidence. She felt as if Dawn was leading her by the hand.

Kite reached up, tilted the heavy book over the shelf edge, eased it down with both hands and returned to her den. A corner of the dust jacket, where the owl's wing should have been, had been ripped away.

She closed the wardrobe, lay down on her bed, propping her head on her pillows, opened the front cover and read the 'Foreword'.

I thought hard about the naming of this book. It has taken me a lifetime to collect together all the photos you see here, and as for my learning about owls, that started when I was just a boy, on the day I met my first 'Little Owl'. He was sitting on a wall near my home in Yorkshire. For a long time I thought the title of this book should be *Owl Knowledge*, but as I added to it, I began to realize that I was accumulating so much more than learning from these magical birds. In the thirty-five years it has taken me to write this book, I have spent hours watching owl behaviour and charting the changes in their lamentably threatened habitats. I have also talked to people from around the world about their extraordinary experiences with owls. I have trawled through folklore and tales from ancient times, and what I have come to learn is that lore, and 'owl lore' in particular, is a kind of learning that goes beyond books, beyond knowledge, beyond observation, beyond logic, beyond traditional 'wisdom' itself to a deeper place of learning within. If this book leads you to listen to their call in the stillness of night as they soar through the darkness to offer you their 'lore', then you would be a fool not to listen.

Anthony Gill
4th June 1962

Kite's hands shook as she turned the pages. She flicked through the pictures of owls in various stages of flight until her eye was caught by a paragraph in the section headed 'Folklore'.

In Celtic legend it is said that the cry of an owl is the cry of a trapped spirit begging to be released. I've been told by many people that owls are used by the dead as a vehicle, to take a message to the living. In Norse legend we find this idea repeated in the figure of the feather-cloaked goddess Freya, who can carry messages between the living and the dead by wearing a coat of feathers, transforming herself into a bird and rising up out of the underworld.

'*You know what they say when a great bird like that flies at you.*' Ellie's words from earlier echoed back at her.

Kite slammed the book closed. Maybe she *was* going mad and needed help . . . to talk to someone; but the person she needed to talk to more than anyone else in the world was Dawn.

Kite Carrec

Kite took the first two steps down the stairs. There was the Dawn owl print, as bright and sharp as ever against another bright blue sky.

'Did you sleep?' Seth asked as she continued down the stairs. He was lounging on the sofa, roof off, guitar by his side, along with an untidy splayed-out mess of papers covered in crossings out and reworkings, which he was just now collecting into a pile. She had the impression that he hadn't slept either.

'Not bad,' Kite lied, edging her way to the opposite end of the sofa and lying down. Her head throbbed with tiredness.

'I was remembering last night when I started teaching you and Dawn the guitar and you would never practise because I suppose you were rebelling, but really, from such an early age, she was always going to be a wonderful musician. I hope to God it wasn't too much pressure for her, getting that scholarship to music school; I thought she was looking forward to it. Did she ever say anything to you?'

'Only that she'd got in,' Kite replied.

Seth wiped the tears from his eyes as he spoke and tried to cover his emotion by tidying up his manuscript papers.

When he'd finished he patted the cushion for Kite to join him at his end of the sofa. She rested her head on his shoulder, following the path of a few wispy clouds meandering like smoke trails high above them.

'You won't believe what Ajay told me about Jack! Sometimes a song will come back to him from his childhood and he can sing the whole thing through word perfect, not a stutter or a stumble.'

'I thought he couldn't speak,' said Kite.

'I know, that's what so incredible, isn't it? Ajay was explaining to me that it's a curiosity of the brain that the songs you sing over and over as a child can be stored in the memory forever.'

Kite wondered if Dawn's Brahms symphony had been stored like that somewhere deep inside her. She could hear her playing right now as swallows darted above them, swelling the sky with life.

'Ajay's going to drop by and see how you're doing later,' Seth said in a throwaway manner. 'I gave him the referral letter from our doctor and he thinks it might be useful for you to see him. Just to make sure you're feeling OK.'

'You had no right to do that!' Kite pushed Seth away sharply as she jumped up off the sofa, her chest tightening with anger. She'd sensed that all this softly, softly stuff was leading to something.

'He can come if he wants to, but I'm NOT talking to him.' She turned her back on Seth and walked towards the window.

'But, Kite, sweetheart, you haven't even cried for Dawn, and you won't talk to any of us. We're worried about you. Isn't that what happened to Dawn, bottling things up and refusing to talk?'

'I don't *know* what happened to Dawn!' Kite shrieked at the top of her voice, slamming her fist into the window. 'I mean, what do you want me to say? Once upon a time I had a best friend and then one day she killed herself, committed suicide, and she's not here any more and then we all lived unhappily ever after. Rubbish story, isn't it? It's easy for her. At least she's dead and can't feel anything. There you go, I've said it, given it a name, which is more than you've had the guts to do.'

Seth's eyes filled with tears again but he didn't try to pursue her as she sprinted to her room, her knuckles burning from the punch. She threw on some running gear and her trainers. Her hands shook as she fumbled with the laces. She ran back down the staircase, ignoring Seth's pleas for her to come back, and headed out of the open entrance of Mirror Falls.

160

She found herself pounding the rocky ground, running downhill by the side of the waterfall, sliding occasionally on the damp rock, letting her feet feel their way as she skidded and leaped over the bony ground. She threw her body forward, accelerating despite her overextended angle to the earth. Dawn's warning cry echoed back at her from the day of the rope-swing accident.

'Be careful, Kite, don't jump. It's too steep!'

If she fell here she would gash open her head on the rock and plunge senseless into the waterfall, but her feet held steadfastly to the path, her heart racing in her chest from this unexpected burst of activity. There was no thought, just the rush of green and rock and branches lashing her face, a ledge and a drop of half her body height, a moment of flying, a heart-leap on to grass littered with sheep droppings. She ran along by the side of the widening stream, feeling the heat of the sun on her back and the sweat trickling down her spine. Now she settled into an even pace, enjoying the stretch of muscle and sinew in her legs, ignoring the feeling of dizziness as her head swam with exhaustion. She began to enjoy the floating sensation, her feet carrying her forward of their own accord. At a turn in the stream she heard the sheepdog's greeting. Now here he was running beside her, occasionally glancing her way. Then he pulled ahead and seemed to be leading her. She followed him up the fell to a small lake nestled in the mountainside. Bardsey ran to the shore where a tiny waterfall cascaded into the lake – and drank thirstily. Kite collapsed on the bank, her heart thudding so loudly she felt as if she was sending a racing heartbeat through the earth, like a roll of thunder. She stared up at the sky, where a gathering of red birds swirled above her head.

The lake was surrounded by an imposing grey crag. Her eyes followed the red birds, whose huge wingspans dominated the sky as they swirled around and around. A vision of Annalisa on her cloud swing entered her head.

The branches in the coppice of trees to her right rustled. She stood up and took a step closer. It was probably a deer: she had read in the guidebook that red deer were common in the area. Then she heard it. Dawn's beautiful playing meandering through the branches, so delicate and soft and warm that it broke her heart to hear it this close.

'I love that.'

'Really? It's something I'm working on for my first concert.'

'Can I come and see you?'

'Yes! But don't tell my mum and dad or they'll invite everyone they know. Just let me get this first one out of the way.'

'Are you nervous?'

'Terrified!'

Dawn's playing seeped into Kite just as it had done at that first concert when Kite had been so proud of her best friend.

Dawn stood between the trees and smiled at her, her fine auburn hair floating on the breeze. Her skin almost transparent. 'I like it here,' she sighed, looking up at the sky . . . 'It's so peaceful. Thanks for bringing me. I know you need me for a while but I can't stay forever. I can always play for you, though.'

Kite nodded, noticing the oboe tucked under Dawn's arm. 'Give me back my golden reed then!' Dawn reached out her hand. Kite felt around in her pocket for the little box and handed it to Dawn. 'My best present ever,' said Dawn, taking out the reed. She walked down to the water's edge and dipped the reed in the lake, attached it to her oboe and began to play. The sound was so rich and tender and golden, it could have made the earth weep.

'There you are, Bardsey!'

Kite tried to lift her head to see where the voice was coming from, but the dog was frantically licking her face. The air felt cool on her skin. She opened her eyes. Everything looked different; the blue had faded and the sun sat low in the sky. She gently pushed the dog away and sat up.

The boy she had seen on the road was staring at her. He looked different close up, less perfect than before. His nose was slightly bumpy over the bridge as if it had been broken. His grey eyes held in them a deep look of concern. Around his neck was a leather necklace with a piece of flat circular slate resting on his collarbone, the grey-blue the same colour as his eyes. Bardsey barked again and bounded at him as if he was a long-lost friend.

'I hope he's not been mithering you?' the boy asked in a soft, low voice.

He was looking at her as if she was an alien that had just landed.

'Did you run all the way up here?'

Kite nodded. 'Why are you staring at me?' she heard herself ask.

'Sorry! Just never thought to come across you here, that's all. Folk aren't usually this adventurous. Are you all right? I mean . . .' He stood awkwardly transferring weight from foot to foot. From what she'd seen of him until now, Kite had imagined him to be more confident, like one of those perfect American high-school boys in films, handsome and golden, glowing with health and motivation.

'Why shouldn't I be all right?'

'No reason! I didn't mean anything by it,' he mumbled.

What was she going to say to this boy who probably already thought she was crazy? That she'd heard her friend, or rather the ghost of her friend, playing the oboe and it had sent her into the deepest sleep she'd had in weeks?

'Do you know what time it is?' she asked.

'Around six o'clock,' the boy answered, looking up at the sun.

Seth would be beside himself with worry. She should get back, but part of her wanted to stay in this place that had given her a feeling of peace. She stood up and walked towards the lake, wondering if any of this was real. She held her hands in the stream of running water and splashed her face several times. Her eyes felt sore and her cheeks stung as the icy water touched her skin.

'Taste it! Freshest spring water you'll drink – some folk think it's got healing powers,' the boy said, coming to her side, cupping his hands together and taking a glug himself. 'So what brings you up here?'

Instead of answering, she dunked her hair into the flowing stream and threw her head back, splashing droplets behind her in a great, glistening rainbow arc. The boy seemed lost for words.

'You've been crying,' he said eventually.

Had she? Kite reached up to her face. That's why her eyes stung – she must have been crying in her sleep. Maybe Dawn had drawn her here to sleep and to cry and perhaps she had a plan, a reason why Kite should meet this awkward boy here too. The strange thing was that now that she was standing so close to him looking out over the flat surface of the lake, something about his quietness and intent listening gaze reminded her of Dawn.

'One of my favourite spots in the Lakes . . . this tarn, well, the whole of Kite Carrec really,' he told her, looking up at the birds wheeling above their heads.

Kite bristled. What were the chances of finding herself in a place that bore her own name? The same place that Jack had shown them in the photo. So these red birds were kites. Grandma Grace would definitely have said that she'd been led here for a reason. Kite reached up for her St Christopher. She had forgotten about it for a while, but the feel of it seemed to bring her back into herself. The boy looked down at the necklace, eased himself away from the rock, picked up a piece of flat slate and started skimming stones across the lake. Ever-increasing circles danced on the flat surface. The boy picked up another slate and handed it to Kite; she threw it flat across the water to form one, two, three, four widening circles. The boy turned and smiled at her. She'd always been good at skimming stones.

Dawn's death had not been a flat pebble. That sort of death would have been something like dying from a random inherited disease. It would have been awful and the ripples would have spread wide across the life of her friends and family, but it would have been better than this. The stone Dawn had lobbed with her suicide had set off explosions in every direction, thought Kite, as she watched the ripples ebb and flow into one another, settling once more into a smooth calm. The ripples of what Dawn had done would stretch out forever, and the water would never feel smooth or still again.

'I'm Garth,' the boy said, interrupting her thoughts. She had almost forgotten he was here. She'd never heard the name before, but it seemed to fit him and this place so well. Looking into his eyes now it was hard to tell exactly what colour they were; in this light they seemed to be more blue than grey.

'I'm Kite,' she managed.

'You're having me on!' Garth laughed. 'You didn't fall from the sky, did you?'

His laughter jarred somewhere deep inside her as it echoed through the valley, as if he was mocking her. There was no way that he could have known how close to the truth his words felt. Above them the red kites sent up a piercing screech. If this was all part of Dawn's plan, she needed to understand how it all pieced together. She stroked Bardsey's head and attempted to gather her thoughts.

'He's Agnes Landseer's dog, isn't he?'

Garth looked a bit taken aback.

'I'm staying at Mirror Falls,' she explained.

'She's my gran; I'm up for the summer.'

So Garth was the beloved grandson that Dr Sherpa had mentioned.

'But she's insane.'

The words flew out of Kite's mouth before she could stop them.

'Is that what folk say?' The sparkle went out of Garth's eyes and he stood up abruptly. 'Come away, Bardsey –' he hesitated for a second– 'unless you need me to walk with you?' he asked as he kicked at the ground in his beaten-up old walking boots.

Kite shook her head. To be honest, she wondered how she would actually make it back to Mirror Falls on her own, but she didn't want him to think that she was weak. After all, how could he know anything about Dawn or how disorientated she felt after sleeping through a whole day? She winced at a sharp shooting pain in her head and watched him walk away.

'She's been leaving notes at our door, that's all!' Kite called after him to offer some sort of explanation for her rudeness, but he had already disappeared into the woods.

Wandering

Her legs felt like steel as she climbed the last stretch of path along the waterfall to find Dr Sherpa's grey Land Rover parked outside Mirror Falls. Now she remembered why she'd run away in the first place.

'So the wanderer returns!' Dr Sherpa was sitting at the kitchen table. He half smiled, half frowned as Kite walked in.

The last thing she needed was to have to explain herself to this stranger. All she wanted now was to take a bath.

'Your dad's been going out of his mind with worry. The police and mountain rescue were about to set out to look for you.'

'Where is Seth?'

'He's just walked to the end of the track to call off the search and to let your mam know you're OK.' Dr Sherpa pointed to the Dawn-owl window. 'We just got in from looking for you and then we saw you ambling back along the stream.'

Kite hesitated at the doorway, wondering if there was any way she might excuse herself.

'You look all worn out. Come and sit down for a moment?' suggested Dr Sherpa, pushing back the chair beside him. He had an authority that was hard to ignore. Now that she'd sat down, her whole body seemed to collapse in on itself.

'So what happened?'

'I went running and then I fell asleep and the next thing I knew it was evening,' Kite replied truthfully.

'Aha! And how are you feeling now?' Dr Sherpa asked, looking into Kite's eyes. She felt that he would see straight through her if she lied.

'I don't know,' Kite answered.

'You know that your dad's told me what happened to your friend,' Dr Sherpa continued. 'I am very sorry indeed.'

Kite shrugged.

'I was concerned to hear that you haven't been sleeping or eating properly, but it's a very good sign, you sleeping all day. Not that I would have recommended it in this way – a gentle walk might have been better,' he smiled, indicating her running gear, 'but the exercise might have done the trick.' What would he have thought if she'd told him that it was really Dawn that had found a way of getting her to sleep by playing her music?

'You will probably find that you feel even more

exhausted for a while,' he continued. 'You've got a lot of catching up to do. The more you sleep, the more you'll need to sleep. For a doctor I have never been very keen on pills. If you ask me, sleeping, eating, exercising and talking are the best medicine in the world!' There was something slightly hypnotic about the slow and steady way he spoke. 'Of course, you must be prepared: your dreams may be troubled, but that's the mind's way of trying to process everything.'

Dr Sherpa stood up from the table and peered down the path to see if Seth was coming. 'I know you don't want to talk to me, and that's fine, but you must find some way of letting your feelings out,' he said.

Kite stared down at the table. When she didn't reply he paced up and down the stepping-stone bridge as if he was searching for the right words.

'I'd forgotten what an extraordinary house this is. You would never guess how many tons of concrete they had to mix to weight the building down at this end enough for it to balance.' He stomped his foot on the ground as he spoke. 'Sometimes I think that it's a bit like that, growing up. You need to have a sturdy foundation so that you can go out into the world and face whatever's in your path . . .'

Kite closed her eyes and sighed sleepily. But his talk of foundations took her back to a project she and Dawn had done at school in RE. They'd had to draw a picture of themselves and then surround their self-portrait with all the elements that made them who they were. It had been one of the few pieces of homework Kite had found easy. She'd included kites and flying, and Dawn's name and a photo of them both, and school and the trapeze and Grandma Grace; she'd done a drawing of Ruby dancing and Seth's guitar, her orange door and the birds of paradise . . . she would have added more but she ran out of space. She had been so surprised when Dawn had called around asking for help with her assignment. It had nearly always been the other way around.

She remembered because of Miss Evans's comment in class. 'You've written what subjects you like at school, not what makes you tick! The question I'm asking is what makes you Dawn? What's at the core of you?' That's all she had said, but Kite had been shocked to see Dawn's eyes filling up with tears. Miss Evans had noticed too and swiftly changed the subject.

'What does she want me to write?' muttered Dawn after class. 'How am I supposed to know what's at the core of me?'

These tiny moments between them were starting to stack up in Kite's brain, and it seemed strange to her now that she had never thought to ask Dawn why she got so upset about the smallest criticism.

Kite heard Seth running up the track behind her. She stood up from the table and turned to him.

'Sorry!'

'Never do that to me again. I can't tell you what was going through my mind . . . It's nearly dark – where in hell's name have you been?' His voice trembled as he strode towards her and enfolded her in his arms, squeezing her so tightly she thought he would never let go.

Kite lay in bed and listened to the two men's low concerned voices echoing up to her from the kitchen below. She had the oddest sensation that they were talking about someone else. The Kite who inhabited this new aching body was unrecognizable even to herself from the person who had once been strong enough to win a half-marathon and train for hours on the trapeze.

The voices moved outside the building.

'I'll call to see her again soon!' Dr Sherpa shouted over the din of the waterfall.

Kite sensed that he was the kind of person who once he made a connection with you would not let go. But what he had said about sleep bringing more sleep seemed to be true. Kite yawned and walked over to the bookshelf, pressed the remote and rummaged underneath her den pillows for the reed box, her feather and her birthday card. And, cradling her Dawn treasures close, her eyes grew heavy.

Stepping Stones

Garth knocked on the glass. His mouth moved as he held a hessian sack up to the window. Something stirred inside it.

'My gran sent this. She says you must not try to follow it.'

First one graceful cream wing appeared and then another. An owl with Dawn's heart-shaped face fluttered out and landed in front of the window, staring in. Then it turned and flew off in the direction of the path under Mirror Falls.

Kite ran to the stepping-stone bridge and peered down to the rock platform below. Crack! The glass shifted and gave way under her.

She was falling, arms and feet splayed in all directions, bones and feathers cascading through ice-cold water, spiralling down, limbs flailing, careering head first towards the gully floor. The owl was screeching and screeching . . .

Kite jerked awake only seconds before she smashed into the ground and clasped her hands over her ears. Seth placed his arms around her shoulders. He was crouched uncomfortably against the back wall of the wardrobe.

174

'What are you doing in here?'

'I could ask you the same question! I came in to say goodnight and found you hiding away. You kept this quiet. What a wardrobe!' He smiled. 'You were sleeping so soundly I didn't want to move you in case I woke you up.'

'What time is it?' Kite asked, squinting into the light.

'Nearly dawn,' he said, then winced at the sound of her name. He sat up and tried to unfold his long body in the confined space. His neck clicked.

'You shouldn't have slept in here all night. I was fine on my own.'

'That's just it,' Seth explained. 'I wanted you to see that you're not alone in all this.'

A high-pitched screech propelled him out of the den on his hands and knees and towards the spyhole window.

'It's the owls,' Kite explained. 'I've been reading about their different cries in a book.'

'It gets under your skin a bit though, doesn't it?' Seth said, as he stretched from side to side and walked through to the bathroom. 'I'm going to need a long hot bath this morning!'

As Kite rearranged her den she quickly gathered up her precious Dawn treasures and carried them over to her bed, tucking them under the bottom fold of her pillowcase. Now that Seth had discovered her hideaway there was no point in keeping them there.

So just as Dr Sherpa had predicted, sleep had brought sleep, however disturbed. Maybe years of listening to Seth's interpretations had washed off on her, because now here she was desperately trying to analyse her dream. Releasing that owl seemed to be saying that she had to set the bird free. Then there was the warning shot about not following Dawn – that probably came from Agnes's weird note – and the spiralling down, well, that's what she'd been doing since the Falling Day. No matter how weird, the dream had strengthened her conviction that Agnes, Garth and the Dawn owl were all bound up together in this. She just had to find out how.

A memory of Garth's hurt expression at the lake returned to her, and she resolved to seek him out to say sorry. Looking back on how rude she'd been about his gran, she felt ashamed of herself. Why had she pushed away the first person she'd actually felt a moment's peace with? She wished she could go back to the lake again to hear Dawn's music. It was Dawn who had led her there and Dawn who had made her understand that there was no need to feel guilty about wanting to see Garth again, because she had brought them together in the first place. If only she knew why.

Bonny Lass

'You can't just have fallen asleep. For all that time?'

Seth was pacing up and down the living room insisting that she ran through the account of yesterday once more.

'So this boy you met, Agnes Landseer's grandson – what was he like?'

'How do I know? I only met him for a few minutes. He seemed all right,' she said, trying to look as disinterested as possible.

'And you ran all the way there, with the dog following you?'

Kite sighed deeply. 'What happened to me is that I fell asleep. Everyone's been going on about how they think it'll be good for me to sleep, and then I do sleep for hours and now you're worried about me sleeping for too long.'

'OK, OK. We won't say any more about it. Just spend the day with me today, please. I've arranged to pick up Jack.' Kite groaned. 'It's just for one day, Kite, Ruby's coming tomorrow so you and she can have a proper talk.'

Kite's head whirred. Ruby's laser vision was all she needed now.

'He's taking us to show me where some of the Storey family once lived. You know they had to flood the whole valley to make the reservoir provide enough water for Manchester. The old village is usually underwater, but because of the drought we're actually going to get to walk the dry reservoir. I tell you, I'm feeling so many songs simmering away . . .' Seth placed his precious guitar in its case.

'You'd better call Rubes,' he said as they drove down the track. 'She was worried sick about you.'

Jack was sitting in a chair outside the Carrec Arms when they arrived. He was wearing his green tweed jacket and matching cap, despite the heat of the morning sun. On his lap he had the little black-and-white photograph of a line of children perched on a wall.

'Ready, Jack?' Seth asked, swinging open the car door and helping him into the front seat as Ellie appeared at the pub entrance with a little posy of wild flowers.

'Will this do you for, Grandad?' she asked, handing it to him. He patted her hand in thanks. 'He's been sat there waiting for you for two hours past. I've not seen him so keen to get out in ages.' Ellie handed Seth a map. 'He's had me up half the night, marking out where he wants to take you. Look! I'd love to come along, but we can't afford to close up at this time of year, with all the thirsty campers and walkers passing through. He maybe won't get out of the car, but he'll enjoy the ride no doubt.'

Seth handed the map to Jack and the old man tapped on a red circle with the number one written inside it. Seth studied the roads and set off through the hamlet.

'I don't suppose there's any point in asking Boss-Nav!' Seth joked, turning to Kite. She forced herself to raise a smile. The least I can do is not drag him down, she thought.

At first there was silence as Jack kept glancing over at Seth, then tracing his fingers along the row of children in the photo, pausing over a little girl with long fair hair. Jack opened his mouth to say something and closed it again. Twice he tapped his head as if that would help to get the information out. Seth kept glancing Jack's way as he drove along the narrow lanes, but when no words came he eventually put on a CD and began humming along to the harmony.

'This is one of mine. What do you think, Jack?'

The old man raised his good hand in a 'so-so' gesture that made Seth laugh.

At first Kite couldn't tell where the crackly but tuneful sound was coming from. Seth switched the CD off, and the old man's mouth moved as his right hand tapped his knee. Seth looked around at Kite in amazement.

179

'There was a bonny lass
Sat upon a stile
I said to yonder lass
Will we walk a while?
Will we walk a while?
O'er fell and stream?
Then the bonny lass
Broke into my dream
There was a bonny lass
I walked her to her door
I said to yonder lass
Will we walk some more?
Will we walk some more?
Fall in step with me
For you and me, my lass
Were surely meant to be
I saw a bonny lass
Sit upon a stile
I said to yonder lass
Will we walk a while?'

As the song came to an end Jack laughed gleefully at the sound of his own voice.

'Are you sure it's OK for me to record your old childhood songs and maybe make something new from them?'

Jack gave Seth a thumbs-up sign.

'I've already got a title: "Song of Storeys".'

Headstones

Kite's forehead knocked against the neck of Seth's guitar. As she opened her eyes it took her a moment to orientate herself, until she registered that it was Jack sitting in the front seat, his car door thrown open.

'I'll just go and see where Seth is,' Kite muttered, but then realized that Jack was fast asleep too, his head lolling as he wheezed heavily in his sleep.

They were parked outside a tiny stone church that backed on to open fields. Seth stood at the far end of the graveyard among the headstones. Why had he brought her here? As if she needed to walk among the dead! But as soon as she entered she felt that there was something peaceful and spacious about the place; so different from the bleak concrete church yard where Dawn had been buried. 'I like it here.' Dawn's soft voice filled her mind. Then it came to Kite, like a revelation, as the delicate wild summer flowers brushed against her calf. What if she could give Dawn a proper burial, somewhere beautiful?

Seth was resting against a large gravestone shaded by the dense canopy of an enormous arching tree. He had taken out a notebook and was scribbling something down.

'What are we doing here?' Kite asked.

'I think Jack's trying to tell me that there's a lot you can work out by reading the names and dates on headstones.'

'They don't tell you *how* people died though, do they?' Kite said, catching sight of a small stone that read:

Alice Liddle (1882–1898) Our angel.

'She was sixteen too!'

Seth looked up from his notebook at Kite's dejected tone.

'I'm sorry, my love,' he said.

Jack coughed loudly, making them both jump. He was clinging on to the wall but now left its security and limped towards them, his left side dragging slightly. He began to run his fingers over the lettering on the headstones as if he was looking for one in particular. Then he tapped Kite's shoulder and pointed to a tiny blue butterfly that fluttered between the stones, coming to rest on a mossy grave. He took a couple of paces to his left, where the butterfly was still basking in the sun, and tapped on the stone. The lichen-covered names and dates were so faded that Seth had to scrape away the moss before reading.

'Storey!' he exclaimed and read the inscription: '*Lily Storey "Dear friend" (1928–1988)*'

Jack traced his stick over the name 'Lily' and then pointed it back at Seth and Kite.

'Do you think she might have been related to my mum?' Jack nodded twice, to make sure Seth knew he was certain. 'Are you saying she was my grandma?' Seth was breathless with excitement.

Jack nodded and tapped the side of his head in frustration as if he would have loved to tell them more, but after a moment he planted his walking stick firmly in the ground and shuffled down a path to another group of headstones further away. Kite and Seth followed him. Leaning on his stick, Jack reached into his pocket and took out the wilting posy Ellie had given him and placed it in Kite's hand. She walked around the graves and tried to read the stones. Jack coughed loudly and she stopped. She could just make out the lettering: '*In Loving Memory of Joyce Salkeld (1918–1978)*'.

'Your wife?' Kite whispered.

Jack nodded as his eyes glazed over with emotion and Kite bent down to place the posy on the grave for him.

On the way out of the churchyard Jack leaned on Kite's arm and she braced herself against his slight weight. Even as exhausted as she was, she could feel the strength in her own body compared to Jack's, but as he hummed a happy tune, Kite wondered whose spirit was stronger at this moment.

'I thought maybe I could give you lunch at Mirror Falls, my way of saying thank you,' Seth suggested when they were back in the car, but Jack turned red in the face and began to cough uncontrollably. Even the water Seth offered him to sip didn't seem to help, so they had no choice but to cut short their tour and head back to the Carrec Arms. What was it about Mirror Falls and Agnes Landseer that troubled Jack so much?

Dry Dam

'I could sit and talk to Jack all day. It's weird, isn't it? If I hadn't come here with you, Kite, Jack's songs could have been lost forever. Ellie says she's never seen them written down anywhere.'

It was a longer drive to the Haweswater Dam than it appeared on Jack's map. Seth seemed thoughtful on the way, caught up in his own thoughts.

As they travelled along a narrow winding lane Kite caught glimpses of a valley off to her right that contained ruins of old walls and buildings.

'So, according to the map, this is it!' Seth announced, pulling up in a dirt car park surrounded by drystone walls. It was quite literally the end of the road. They got out, walked to a stile and climbed over. Sheep ambled close by, unconcerned by their presence. A scattering of people were taking various tracks down to the bottom of the dam, as if there was an unwritten code that no one should stray too close to each other. Just like me and Seth, Kite mused, wandering aimlessly along random paths, never walking the same thought track. As if to contradict her, Seth took her hand as they continued to scramble downhill and over the ruins of a bridge leading to a crumbled boundary wall.

'To think we could be standing in the house where Jack or my grandparents grew up,' Seth pondered as they trudged over the rubble. 'Sad, in a way, that all this history's usually underwater. Imagine finding out that the village where your family have lived for generations has to be flooded to make a reservoir to supply water for somewhere as far away as Manchester. They must have felt like sacrificial lambs . . .'

While Seth was absorbed in picturing his ancestors, Kite looked around at the barely visible remnants of walls. There wasn't much to see, as far as she was concerned. Then a loud bark pierced the air and Bardsey bounded up to her, throwing his paws against her chest and knocking her off her feet.

'That dog gets everywhere!' Seth laughed.

Kite dusted her clothes off and sat up. 'What are you doing so far away from home?' she asked, stroking Bardsey's soft head. The dog seemed to have a real affection for her; she wondered if he could sense how sad and lonely she was.

Bardsey ran back to a huddle of walkers who were gathered around some kind of sculpture rising above a drystone wall. Next to the sculpture stood Garth, holding a trowel. Bardsey trotted over to him and nuzzled his head into his side. Garth looked up at Kite without smiling and continued his work.

The other walkers wandered away so that now the sculpture came clearly into view. It was formed from a whole sheep's carcass. Could this be the one Kite had seen under Mirror Falls?

Seth frowned with concentration as he stepped closer to watch Garth work. 'Mind if I have a look?'

Garth opened his arms as if to say, 'Be my guest.'

Seth approached the sculpture, which sat within the confines of a wall made of layers and layers of slate and stone jigsawed together. 'What's this?' he asked, indicating the boundary that surrounded the structure.

'It's called a garth – a sheepfold. I've looked at old maps of the farm and rebuilt it in the same place that the original would have been.' Seth nodded appreciatively. Kite supposed in their own way they were both retracing the history of the valley.

Kite hung back on the outside of the walled area, wishing that Seth would leave them alone for a few moments so that she could apologize for what she'd said about Agnes. The weird thing was that because she'd thought so much about Garth, even dreamed of him, she felt as if she knew him so much better than she did. But now, watching him work on this sculpture, she realized she knew nothing about him at all. Why would he want to make a sculpture out of bones? It must have taken him ages to reconstruct the skeleton. Where the stomach would once have been he had wedged tiny pieces of flint forming a curved drystone belly within the ribcage.

'Did you get this from under Mirror Falls?' Seth asked.

'Aye, Agnes found it.' It made Kite shudder to think of Agnes Landseer rummaging around underneath the house.

'So you're Agnes Landseer's grandson.' Seth looked from Kite to Garth. 'You two have already met then. Aren't you going to introduce me, Kite?'

'Seth, this is Garth,' Kite mumbled.

'Garth – and you're making a garth! You could call this a sort of signature piece then?' Seth laughed.

Garth smiled at him and carried on working.

'What are those?' Seth asked, peering in between the cracks.

'Found things, and stuff folk have brought me off the fells.' Garth shrugged. 'That woman I was just talking to, she brought me this baby's clog.' Garth reached forward and placed it in Kite's hand without even asking if she wanted to see it. It was no bigger than her palm.

'That could have belonged to my grandma,' Seth began to examine the other objects lodged between the sheep's bones: cotton bobbins, rusty old horseshoes, coins, sheep's wool, tiny yellow-white teeth, old nails, broken pieces of pottery and knitting needles. He examined every object as if they were clues to a complicated puzzle.

'And it'll all be washed away when the reservoir fills up again?'

'We'll see . . . I've built it fairly sturdy though. Anyway, that's sort of the point.' Garth smiled again.

Seth looked at Garth and held out his hand. Why was Seth being so weird? He hardly ever shook hands with anyone.

'I see you've inherited your grandmother's artistic eye.' Seth walked to the front of the sculpture and stood back to admire it.

Kite cringed, but Garth seemed happy enough to talk about it.

'I just started building, and then folk seemed to be taken by it, and now the newspapers have been down here taking photos and everything.'

'I can see why!' Seth nodded admiringly. 'I'm just going to have a bit of a wander.'

After he had walked away Garth kicked a few pieces of loose slate under his feet and finally looked up at Kite.

'Want to help?'

Kite picked up a handful of slates and stepped inside the wall. He stood on the other side of the sheep looking through its bones at her with his piercing eyes.

'Don't you think it's all a bit grim?' Kite asked as she began placing tiny shards of slate in the ribcage of the sheep. She could hear the tone of her voice, and she wished she could have found something kinder to say.

'Not really – it's just the natural cycle of things, is how I see it,' Garth answered. She wondered what he would say if she told him about Dawn. How could what Dawn had done fit into any natural cycle?

'I'm sorry!' Kite blurted, as she wedged in another piece of slate. 'For what I said – about your gran.'

'It's nowt others haven't thought.' He shrugged. 'You were upset. But she's my gran, and if you got to know her, you wouldn't think badly of her.'

They worked silently for a while. As she placed slate after slate inside the sheep carcass Kite wondered what it would take for her to change her opinion of Agnes Landseer.

'Are you ready to go?' Seth called over to Kite. 'I expect we'll see you again, Garth,' he added.

'I hope so,' Garth spoke the words softly, as if they were meant only for Kite.

'Got something about him, that boy,' Seth said as he opened his car door and turned back to watch him working. 'A sort of grand humility. I like that – what do you think of that as a lyric: "grand humility".'

'It's good,' agreed Kite as she looked down over the

190

valley where Garth seemed little more than a spot on the landscape.

Seth drove along, humming the tune that Jack had sung earlier. As they meandered along the winding lanes Kite closed her eyes and tried to piece together what she'd seen of Garth. Now she was certain. The way he said so little while tuning into everything around him definitely reminded her of Dawn. It was not until now that she'd realized how much of the talking she had always done, and how much she had relied on Dawn to listen.

The Reed Box

As soon as they got back to Mirror Falls Kite retreated to her bedroom. She went over to her pillow and took out her Dawn treasures. Her hands paused on the birthday-card. If Hazel had not already told her that there were no final words, no confiding explanations inside, she would have ripped the envelope open straight away. Why was she keeping it? What good could it do? And yet her hands shook as she turned the card over and slipped it back inside the folds of her pillowcase.

The feather and the reed were the sorts of thing that Garth might weave into his sculpture, thought Kite. She took out Dawn's golden reed. The natural bamboo would fit perfectly between the tiny shards of slate, and the golden thread might catch your eye and draw you to it. Seth had been right about Garth when he'd said that there was something deep in what he was doing. There were secrets and stories in these objects. How many precious things had she and

Dawn talked of as she'd watched her work away at her delicate reeds? She smoothed her fingers over the fine worn ends. Dawn had loved the sound it made so much that after it was worn out she'd bound it together with golden silken thread and from time to time even soaked it in water as if she hoped that one day she would play it again.

'What's this?' Kite asked, holding up a little jam jar full of water.

'I carry that everywhere with me, to soak my reed before I play. If you let them get brittle and dry, they're ruined.'

Kite walked through to the bathroom and washed her hands in lemon soap, just as Dawn always did before she touched her reeds. Then she held the reed under the tap and as the water streamed over it, the seed of an idea that had come to her in the graveyard began to grow. Perhaps Dawn had led her to Garth because he had created the perfect place to bury Dawn's reed. Now she though of it, this was the nearest she would ever get to burying Dawn's body. She held the fine, worn bamboo up to the light, remembering Dawn's description of the reed's heart, spine and voice, but for the reed to 'speak' Kite needed rain. When the dam was full of water, Garth's sculpture would be the perfect resting place for Dawn. It was all clear to her now. She would wait until the weather broke and then take the golden reed down to the reservoir and give

Dawn a proper burial. Kite imagined the water flowing through the reed, playing its own gentle music. She would be able to come back to this place whenever she wanted to be with Dawn. This would be nothing like that wretched mud-puddle burial in London. I need to do this for Dawn . . . to bring her peace, Kite told herself as she clasped the golden reed in her hands, and I need to do it for myself, to let her go.

The Valley of Mist

Back in her room Kite switched on the iPod and lay back to listen to Dawn's playing.

In flew the Dawn owl, wings outstretched and soaring towards her. Kite watched herself screaming, 'Stop! Stop! Stop!' over and over again, but the great bird with Dawn's face kept coming. She pressed her hand against the window as if that could make the owl change her course. The glass fell away beneath her and she was spiralling downward, jagged rock, stone and bone snagging her clothing as she fell. Then a flurry of wings and the soft sound of Dawn's playing and she was being lifted and placed gently on a rock ledge. Beside her lay the carcass of a sheep. She felt someone brush against her arm. She turned, and there, sitting beside her, was Dawn.

'What are you doing here?' Kite whispered.

'Trying to make you understand,' Dawn said, smiling sadly, then looking up to the path where Garth was standing watching them both. He was holding Dawn's reed.

'What's this?' he asked, inspecting it.

Kite turned back to Dawn, but she seemed to have melted into the water. Only her lemon smell lingered.

'That was Dawn's heart, her spine and her voice,' Kite whispered.

She woke to the sound of a girl sobbing.

'Dawn!' she called out, but there was no answer.

She stumbled down the staircase and stared through one of the glass stepping stones, hypnotized by the force of the waterfall that surged beneath her feet.

Kites circling round and round
Water falling
Kite's falling
Dawn's face
Tears falling
Feathers falling
Music in the air
Driftwood floating
Reeds circling
Around and around and around and around . . .

Someone was stroking their fingers over her scar-brow as if to smooth the hurt away. There was only one person in the world who did that.

'You said she was doing well!' Ruby's voice was shrill with shock.

Kite felt herself being lifted and laid down on a sofa. 'I'll call Dr Sherpa from the end of the track!' Seth yelled back from the kitchen, and she heard his car rumble away.

She hardly dared open her eyes to face the barrage of questions, but when she did Ruby simply enveloped her in her arms and the warmth of her cinnamon perfume and rocked her to and fro.

'My darlin', I got such a shock when I saw you lying on the ground like that. What happened?'

'I was just running downstairs, slipped on the glass and hit my head,' Kite explained, reaching up to her forehead and feeling an egg-shaped bump.

'The doctor will be here in a while. You should try to stay awake till then.' Ruby fussed around her, placing an icy flannel on Kite's bruise. 'So tell me! What's all this about an architect and her grandson?'

Kite shrugged. For a moment the image of Garth reaching out to her in her dream flashed through her mind. She wondered why, out of all the people she had met, she had entrusted him with Dawn's precious reed, even if it was only in a dream . . .

Ruby followed Kite's gaze up towards the owl print.

'There must be a way to get rid of that,' Ruby took a step closer to the glass.

'Not unless it rains.'

'No sign of that.' Ruby smiled, pointing up at the endless cornflower-blue sky.

There was no way to explain to Ruby how much Kite wished for rain. If she told Ruby that the owl that crashed into the window had worn Dawn's face, she would probably make them pack up and leave today. Kite knew that she would have to work hard to put Ruby's mind at rest, because whatever happened now, she had to stay here till the weather changed. Something settled deep inside her. It felt as if she'd made a promise to Dawn that she had to keep.

'So how's the fell runner?' Dr Sherpa called through from the kitchen as he made his way to her side. 'You must be Ruby.' He shook hands with her and Kite noticed a wry smile cross his face as he noticed her colourful nails.

'And I've heard such wonderful things about you, Dr Sherpa,' Ruby said.

'Please, call me Ajay.'

'Can I get you a cup of tea or coffee?'

'Tea would be grand. Just milk, please, Ruby.'

Dr Sherpa laid his hand on Kite's forehead and took her temperature. He felt her pulse and got her to stick out her tongue. Then he asked her to count how many fingers he was holding up. 'No dizziness or blurred vision?'

Kite shook her head.

'Physically you're fine, no damage done,' Dr Sherpa lowered his voice. 'But how are you feeling in here?' He tapped his chest and then his head. She knew what he meant.

She shrugged.

'I knew a young lad once from around here, took his

own life. I brought him into this world and he seemed such a contented boy. Devastated that family, it did.'

'But why . . . ?' The question flew from her mouth. It was little more than a whisper.

Dr Sherpa smoothed his hand over his forehead and face as if to wipe away the memory of the family's pain.

'People don't talk much about depression in the young, but they should because it's more common that you would think. Everyone expects you to be happy and full of life, but it can come upon people at any age. Life can throw some tough challenges at you.'

'Do you think Dawn was depressed?'

'I think she must have been. By the sound of it.'

'But I was her best friend and I didn't have a clue.' Kite found the sound of herself talking about Dawn strange.

'Do you think I'm depressed?' she asked the doctor.

'Certainly traumatized by your friend's suicide. But the way you feel is understandable after what's happened, and at least we're all aware of it. What your friend had was probably something more long-term. Even so, I think when you get back home you should definitely try and speak to the counsellor, the way you're starting to talk to me.'

Dr Sherpa stared out of the window. 'Have you seen how the morning mist settles down there in the valley?'

Kite nodded.

'Depression feels a bit like that, it creeps in on you and settles, until you think it'll never lift, but in time it nearly always does. That's why it's so tragic if people don't reach out to anyone when they feel low, because if they do, the mist will usually lift in the end.'

Kite felt that since she'd stepped on to this hanging glass barge she had been floating through that valley of mist, but now that she knew what she had to do for Dawn, maybe it would start to lift.

She woke to the homely smell of Ruby's cooking.

'Hungry?' Ruby asked, smiling at her daughter's wild hair and sleepy eyes as she wandered into the kitchen.

'I come bearing mangoes from Manchester, and I've cooked up a Spanish omelette!' Ruby tipped it from the sizzling pan on to a plate. Kite's stomach rumbled as she took a thick slice. Ruby settled next to her and watched contentedly as Kite ate.

'Where's Seth?'

'Gone off to look up records! He's trying to find confirmation that his grandmother was Lily Storey. I think what he really wants to know is why his mum was adopted. I just hope he knows how steeped in secrecy these things can be.'

Kite pictured her unopened birthday card under her pillow. Was it better to know?

Dance

'How did I get up here!' Kite asked, opening her eyes and peering around the bedroom.

'Seth carried you. After you ate you crashed out on the sofa again. You didn't even stir when he picked you up. So, I see you haven't flown your new kite.' Ruby brought it through to her bedroom and hung it from a hook on the wall. 'I can't believe you haven't even unpacked it yet!'

'I didn't know we'd brought it,' Kite mumbled, staring at the bright colours against the stone wall. She was glad that Ruby had come.

The intoxicating smell of her nail varnish filled the room.

'What do you think?' Ruby held her nails up to the light. 'Green and silver with a touch of purple . . . homage to the Cumbrian countryside!'

Kite laughed. It was what she loved about Ruby, the randomness of her, the fact that she seemed to get so much pleasure out of something as small as painting her nails.

'Want me to do yours?'

Kite nodded and held out her hands. While Ruby was concentrating on applying the varnish in smooth layers, Seth came sprinting up the glass staircase.

He stood in the doorway, smiling at the scene before him.

'Now that's something I haven't seen for a while . . . Am I interrupting?'

'Yes!' answered Ruby without looking up.

He ignored her, strolled over and sprawled out at the opposite end of the bed, so that he was facing them both.

'Well, did you find anything?' asked Ruby.

Seth shook his head. 'According to the records, Lily's two sisters and her brother are accounted for. Lily was the only one who lived here all her life, but she never married and she died here too. That *was* her grave Jack led us to the other day.'

'You know, if your mum was given to a children's home, there's a good chance the birth might have been covered up,' Ruby warned.

'Maybe I'll just have to accept that I'll never know. The irony is that the person who could probably tell me can't even talk!'

It felt to Kite as if Seth was talking about Dawn. What if there was no way of uncovering exactly why she had ended her life, no way of knowing what she had been thinking and feeling at that moment? Kite peered into Seth's dejected face. For the first time since Seth had set out on this family-history journey she began to understand how much this search meant to him. They were both looking for answers from beyond the grave.

'Can't Jack write it down?' Ruby asked.

Seth shook his head. 'The stroke's affected his coordination. Anyway, his hands are rigid with arthritis.'

'Poor old man,' Ruby sighed as she delicately layered the silver varnish on to Kite's nails.

Seth brightened suddenly. 'As you're doing yourselves up I thought I'd take my girls out on the town . . . well, not exactly town! I've got a gig in the Carrec Arms.'

'Didn't take you long to get in with the locals,' Ruby laughed.

'I'm family now, you know. If only I could work out how!' Seth grinned.

'I wonder if they'll accept me into their fold.'

'What do you mean?' asked Kite, surprised. Ruby was usually so self-confident.

'They'll love you! Everyone does,' Seth assured her.

'I hope so! I started getting the countryside stare somewhere north of Lancaster!'

Kite laughed as Ruby blew on her nails.

'It's no different than when I first went to St Kitts,' Seth insisted. 'I thought Grace would treat me like a tourist, but she made me feel at home straight away! It's the same here. We're all family, and you two belong in the Lake District as much as I do!'

Seth seemed to want Ruby to love this place as much as he'd loved St Kitts. Kite supposed it was because, apart from her and Ruby, these people were the nearest thing he had to family. Kite saw now that this thing of 'belonging' that Dawn had fretted over was more important than she'd ever appreciated. Maybe the more connections you had with the world, the harder it was to break those ties.

'Anyway, Dr Sherpa's been one of the locals for years.' Seth leaned over and kissed Ruby, and she kissed him back.

'Don't mind me,' Kite groaned, but it felt good to be all together again. 'How long are you staying?'

The smile faded from Ruby's face. 'Darlin', I have to be back in Manchester tomorrow, but you're welcome to come with me.'

Kite shook her head decisively.

'Well, then the least I can do is yam up the freezer with food for you. You're looking too skinny, my girl.'

Seth placed a comforting hand on Ruby's back. 'Right, I'm off to get a bit of practice in.'

From upstairs they listened to him strumming away at a song that was familiar to Kite, except that he'd added a harmony that softened it and made it sound more contemporary.

> 'There was a bonny lass
> Sat upon a stile
> I said to yonder lass
> Will we walk a while?
> Will we walk a while?
> O'er fell and stream?
> Then the bonny lass
> Broke into my dream
> There was a bonny lass
> I walked her to her door
> I said to yonder lass
> Will we walk some more?
> Will we walk some more?
> Fall in step with me
> For you and me, my lass
> Were surely meant to be.'

'That's a new one! It's catchy. I like it,' Ruby called down the stairs.

'Actually it's pretty ancient,' Seth called back.

The Gig

Kite felt oddly self-conscious getting dressed up. She dabbed foundation on the egg-shaped bump above her scar-brow, but then glancing in the mirror, she thought it looked worse.

She was wearing her denim miniskirt with one of Ruby' silk scarves threaded around her waist to hold it up. She'd chosen a purple tie-dye T-shirt and her dirty once-white Converse. Ruby had given her a few plaits in the side of her hair and drawn it back into a loose knot. Kite felt like pulling them out because she could hide her bruise better without them, but she didn't want to upset Ruby and so the plaits stayed.

'There's my beauty!' she said. 'Want to wear some earrings?' Kite shook her head. She already felt over the top with her painted nails.

They'd trundled halfway down the pot-holed track when Kite insisted on stopping. She almost let it slip that the only reason she needed to go back was to close the blinds, but she could do without getting into a conversation with Ruby about Agnes. Without discussing it, Seth and Kite had kept quiet about her notes, despite the fact that Ruby had commented several times that it was gruesome to see the owl's markings splayed out against the window. If she thought that there was a crazy old woman writing notes to Kite, she might insist that she get on the train back to Manchester with her. So Kite made up the excuse of feeling cold and that she needed to go back in to grab her jacket.

'You could have thought of that before,' complained Ruby.

When she'd run into the house and come back out again without it, Ruby had looked at her as if she was deranged.

'I'm not cold any more.' Kite shrugged.

'You can always borrow my pashmina. Let's make a move then. I haven't seen anything of this countryside yet, except for this weird house.'

'I thought you'd like it, Rubes,' said Seth, looking a bit put out.

'The views are to die for and I wouldn't mind that wardrobe in Kite's bedroom, but as Grandma Grace would say, "Eh, eh! Spiritless and fanciful."' Ruby winked at Kite in the back seat.

Kite smiled to herself and held on to Grandma Grace's St Christopher. Ruby was full of contradictions. For someone who professed not to believe in all of Grace's 'spirit talk', Ruby had surprisingly strong reactions to places and people.

They stopped at the stream and let their feet drift in the water, just as Kite had done on the first day. The air was full of the sweet fresh smells of harvest. Round bales of straw were dotted around the nearby fields and strands of hay floated loose on the light summer breeze. Kite picked her way over rocks and stones to the pool in which she'd seen Dawn's face emerge from the swirling mass of minnows. She hardly dared look as a few tiny fish shone in the evening sun, darting in and out between mossy stones, but this time no face appeared.

'I can't believe how lucky you've been with this weather.' Ruby sighed with pleasure, leaning back on a large boulder and offering her face up to the warmth of the sun. She was wearing a deep red sleeveless dress with a mustard pashmina around her shoulders and her ebony necklace with the enormous beads that they'd bought together in St Kitts. Her plaited hair was twisted into an elegant pile on the top of her head.

They parked the car at the beginning of the hamlet, so that Ruby could have a nose around the tiny stone cottages. As they walked the rest of the way to the pub a gaggle of geese wandered up the road stopping to stretch their necks, noses down, hoovering up any traces of food. That, thought Kite, as she listened to the geese and their high-pitched honking, was the sound that Dawn used to make when she first blew out a reed. She was always a bit embarrassed about the ugliness of the noise. Maybe if she'd done the same with her feelings, told someone about everything from her most ridiculous-sounding worries to her bitterest thoughts, she might have been able to carry on with life. Kite shook herself. That was the problem. It seemed that all the things she saw around her; even a gaggle of geese walking down a lane, could lead her back to Dawn.

'Well, this is the venue of my debut Lakeland gig!' announced Seth, stopping outside the Carrec Arms.

'Duck!' shouted Seth too late, as Ruby clonked her head on the low beam and stumbled inside.

Jack was standing behind his chair staring straight at Ruby as Seth walked over to him.

'This is Ruby, and *this* is Jack.' Seth ushered Ruby over as he spoke.

'I've heard all about you.' Ruby smiled, rubbing her head.

Jack reached towards her in concern.

'It's nothing!' she said, shaking his hand enthusiastically.

Jack took hold of Ruby's hand and ran his fingers over her skin and down to her fingers and smiled. Her decorated nails seemed to amuse him.

Ellie came over from the bar. She had dressed up

for the occasion too, wearing a pretty sky-blue print dress gathered in at the waist. Her hair tumbled in ringlets down her back.

'And Ellie!' Seth smiled.

'You're very welcome!' Ellie touched Ruby on the arm and invited her to sit down. 'Now what can I get you to drink? I've invited a fair few people, but I'm not sure who'll turn up.'

'I don't mind if no one else comes,' Seth declared. 'As long as I've got an audience!'

He took his guitar out of its case and started playing along to the new arrangement of 'Bonny Lass' he'd been working on the night before. Jack's right hand and foot began tapping along as he hit upon the words and joined in.

Seth had moved on to one of his own songs and Ruby was chatting away to Jack when Dr Sherpa and his wife arrived. Dr Sherpa inclined his head subtly towards Kite, as if to ask her how she felt now. She wished she was invisible. Before . . . she had always been the one to bowl straight into a situation, to chatter away and take everything at face value, happy to be the centre of attention. Now she supposed that she was getting to see the world more as Dawn had done, sitting quietly on the edges and watching everything unfold in front of her.

'How come you always manage to analyse everything that goes on?' Kite asked her when they'd been out late to a party one night and Dawn had started on her usual morning-after autopsy.

'I can't help it!' Dawn sighed.

'That's why you can never enjoy the party properly!' Kite told her.

Dr Sherpa waved at Seth, who continued strumming away as the doctor strolled over to Ruby and Kite and introduced them to Priti, his wife. She *is* pretty thought Kite. She was dressed in a silken sea-green salwar-kameez top, jeans and sparkly sandals. Her hair was drawn into a long loose plait. Within a few minutes the two women were deep in conversation. Once Ruby got going about her passion there was no stopping her, especially when Priti told her how much she loved dance, especially contemporary.

'It's been a while since we've had a "do" in here,' Ellie commented as a stout middle-aged couple walked through the door and greeted them. Kite thought she saw an amused look cross their faces at the eclectic gathering of people.

Seth was halfway through singing an old Calypso song he'd learned in St Kitts when Jack pushed back his chair and stood up slowly without the use of his walking stick. He held out his hand to Ruby. She stood up, taking his good arm, and guided him gracefully around the room. Jack raised his head and his right hand proudly in the air as they danced across the tiny square of stone floor. For a moment it was as if he had forgotten about his numb leg. Everyone else clapped along to the music as Ruby manoeuvred Jack safely once more around the room. Kite loved to see her mother dance. Her whole body lit up and she seemed to draw people to her through the sheer force of her energy. Old Jack and Ruby made good dancing partners. They both had such a passion for life. Where did that sense of joy come from? Could you make someone feel it, or was it just inside you or not? Kite wondered if she would ever get that feeling back.

Jack was laughing breathlessly as Ruby and he bowed to each other formally at the end of the dance. But instead of returning to his seat he walked slowly over to the stairs . . . leaning heavily on his stick now.

'Have you had enough, Grandad? Do you want to rest now?'

Jack reached up to Ellie's face and stroked her cheek.

'I'll take you up.' Dr Sherpa offered Jack his arm for support. Halfway up the ancient oak steps Jack turned and looked down on the scene below as if he was drinking it in.

'Good night, Grandad!' Ellie called up to him.

It seemed to take forever for Ruby and Seth to say their goodbyes so Kite wandered out of the pub ahead of them. She regretted it straight away. A gathering of people about her age were hanging out by the wall outside, a collection of spent cans strewn around their feet.

'Hi!' said the girl with bright pink hair who'd smiled at Kite at the clock tower on their first day. The boy with the leather jacket had his arm swung over her shoulder as they leaned back against the motorbike seat.

'This is Kite!' She recognized Garth's voice straight away as he stood up and stepped forward into the light. He was wearing army trousers and a plain white T-shirt, and the slate necklace she'd seen him in before. He played with it nervously as he drew close enough to her so that the others wouldn't hear him speaking. She pulled out one of her plaits and twisted it around her fingers.

'What happen to your head?' Garth whispered.

Kite raised her hand back up to her scar-brow.

'Not your scar . . . here,' Garth pointed to the raised, bruised skin above her brow and his hand brushed her hair as he did so. Kite's heart fluttered. So he had already looked at her closely enough to notice the scar.

'Oh that, it's nothing, just a bruise! I fell.'

'So this is *the* Kite of Kite Carrec!' The girl with pink hair came over.

'Hi, I'm Cassie,' she said. 'No point waiting for Garth to introduce us.' She nudged Garth's arm playfully. 'Think he wants to keep you to himself.' Garth kicked at the ground and Kite couldn't read the expression on his face.

'Sorry we didn't get here earlier,' Cassie continued. 'We only caught the end. Your dad's really good though.'

'Thanks!' Kite mumbled as Seth and Ruby came bowling out of the pub laughing.

'How's it going, Garth?' Seth called over.

'I've gotta go!' Kite said. She and Ruby dreaded Seth striking up a conversation when they couldn't think of what to say to Garth or the others.

'Maybe see you around?' Cassie called after her. 'Love the nails!'

Kite didn't turn back, but waved as the motorbike revved up behind her. Her face was flushed with embarrassment as she walked away, feeling curious eyes boring into her back.

Prelude

The station was surprisingly busy, considering it was only seven o'clock in the morning. The travellers were an eclectic combination of smartly dressed executives setting off to work in one of the neighbouring cities, students on their way to school or college, serious-looking backpackers carrying ridiculously heavy loads . . . and Ruby. She stepped on to the train and paused in the doorway, facing the platform.

'Sure you don't want to decamp to Manchester?'

Kite shook her head. It had been good to see Ruby, but now she knew she needed to stay and wait for the rain. She could tell by the way Seth had supported her decision that he was desperate to stay here himself. Despite her initial resistance, the landscape and its people seemed to have ignited something in them both.

Ruby winked at Kite as she settled down in her window seat, pressing her hand against the glass and wiggling her elegant fingers in a wave. Seth wrapped an arm around Kite's shoulders as the train pulled away and Ruby mouthed the words, 'Bye, my darlin', love you.'

'Love you too,' Kite mouthed back.

She was used to either Seth or Ruby being away on tour so the raw emotion that threatened to rise up from somewhere deep in her stomach surprised her. It felt as if the tight little knot that she had held inside her for so long was beginning to unravel and with it she was losing control. The tears rose to her eyes. What was wrong with her? She couldn't cry for Dawn, at least not in her waking hours, but she was crying about saying goodbye to Ruby when she would be seeing her again in a few days. Kite rubbed the tears roughly from her eyes.

If only she had been able to say goodbye to Dawn.

'Let's take a drive around the Lakes,' suggested Seth.

On a whim he hired a little boat and fishing rods on the shore of Lake Crummock Water. He'd got it into his head that he wanted to catch a brown trout for Jack. Kite was worried that Seth would try to use the time to talk, but as it turned out, he was so focused on learning how to cast the line without getting it tangled that there wasn't much chance for conversation. Kite stared up at the familiar uninterrupted blue sky and wished for a great wind to scud across, bringing racing clouds of grey and charcoal. She closed her eyes and opened her senses and hoped that Dawn would visit her again in her dreams:

gentle lapping of water against the boat side
reeling in and out of fly rod
zip noise as the line runs
bird call far off
splash
water lapping
lapping
boat rocking from side to side

'Get the net, quick!'

She opened her eyes at the urgency of Seth's voice. A golden brown fish leaped from the water and plummeted back down again, leaving ever-decreasing circles rippling over the surface. Seth let the line run, allowing the fish its freedom, and then slowly he began to tighten his hold and reel it in. Again and again it leaped out of the water, arching upward and swishing its tail this way and that.

'It's putting up a good fight!' panted Seth as he reeled it in closer, his eyes bright with excitement. Kite found herself willing the trout to unhook itself. Then, as Seth leaned over the side of the boat with the net, the fish within touching distance, it made one last attempt to escape, this time diving deep into the dark water below the boat. After a few seconds it floated to the surface on its side, the hook embedded in its mouth as it flicked its tail weakly. Seth scooped the net under the fish, and lifted it in over the side of the boat.

'Look away!' he ordered, but Kite was transfixed as Seth laid the trout out in the deck. She stood, as the boat rocked from side to side, and watched in horror as the fish opened its mouth and gills, gulping air where water should have been. She held her breath as Seth picked up something that resembled a small hammer. He raised his arm in the air and brought it down hard on the trout's head. A tiny trickle of blood oozed from its mouth and it stilled. Seth took some tweezers from the tool box under the seat and carefully removed the hook.

Kite stared.

'*Please* can we just go back?' she whispered. She felt as if someone had hit *her* hard on the back of the head.

Seth reached a hand towards her but she snatched hers away. Her stomach lurched with the horror of seeing life turn to death before her eyes. It was the first time she had ever seen anything die.

The girl at the boat hut provided some newspaper and string and packed the fish with ice from her freezer box to keep it fresh.

'It won't have felt any pain,' Seth assured her as they drove away.

'How do you *know*?'

She had tried not to think about the way Dawn

had died. She hoped more than anything it would have been as Ruby said, without pain, but there was no way of really knowing.

Seth ran into the Carrec Arms brandishing his parcel.

'You'll never guess what I've got for you, Jack!'

Dr Sherpa and Ellie were sitting at the table. Dr Sherpa had a protective arm wrapped around her shoulders. Ellie's eyes were red and swollen. Kite looked over to Jack's empty chair and Dr Sherpa shook his head.

'But I caught him a trout for his supper,' Seth said, sounding like a disappointed child as he placed the fish on the table.

Ellie looked at it blankly.

'What a shame! Jack loved nothing better than a fresh buttered trout for his breakfast,' Dr Sherpa said. The words choked in his throat as he spoke them.

Kite felt the tears sting her eyes and roll down her cheeks. Seth hugged her to him and she looked up to see that he was crying too.

Ellie was telling the story again of how she found Jack, as if she was trying to believe it herself.

'I popped up with a cup of tea this morning and he was gone. The odd thing is, he had a photo of Mirror Falls in his hands. Well, I suppose it was his land and he always loved to go up to that spot on the hill. He was such a fit man, running up there till way after his seventieth birthday.'

It was early afternoon when they left. Seth had gone up to see old Jack and sat with him for what seemed like hours while Ellie talked downstairs. Kite had no desire to see his body. She wanted to remember him as he had been the night before, dancing around the pub with Ruby. At least he'd left everyone with happy memories.

'I'm sorry, Kite' Seth sighed as they got into the car. 'You should have gone back to Manchester with Ruby.'

Kite shook her head.

'So what am I going to do with Jack's fish now?'

'I don't know. Let's just go back,' Kite pleaded.

'It's been a long, sad day,' Seth said. 'I feel shattered myself, and I can't believe it's still only three o'clock.' He checked his watch as he drove across the common to the bottom of the track.

'I'll walk the rest of the way,' Kite said.

'I know how you feel, I'm not ready to go back yet either. Do you mind if I drop you off? I'll only be an hour or so.' Seth handed her the key. 'It's probably a whim, but I caught that trout for Jack and if he can't have it I think I know the perfect place for it.'

'With You in Spirit'

Kite walked up the track and there at the sandstone entrance, weighted down by a pebble, was another note. She winced. The same envelope, the same paper, the same scored-out address.

> Dear Kite,
> I wanted to thank you for pulling
> down the blinds. I spoke to garth
> and I see now that I should have
> explained better. I only ask to protect
> the owls, to stop them flying into the
> window at night. I hope you'll come
> and see me at Scar View with garth.
> I'd like to show you something.
> Agnes Landseer

Kite took the note and placed it on the table with the others. This one was definitely friendlier, but something about that woman still made her feel uncomfortable. What could she possibly want to show her? Kite walked over to the window, where the owl print shone silver in the afternoon sunshine. Now she was alone, the place felt unbelievably empty, as if it had no warmth or heart.

Images of the day flashed through her head: waving Ruby off on the station and feeling as if she was saying goodbye to her forever; the vision of the fish opening and closing its mouth, gulping air and fighting for life; the vacant expression on Ellie's face when they'd entered the Carrec Arms; the tears for Jack. She walked over to the table, picked up Agnes's note, turned it over and wrote.

> Just gone for a walk to think things through.
> I'll be back later. Don't worry about me,
> I'm fine.
> Love Kite X

She left the note on the sandstone slab weighted by the key and walked down the steep path that led away from Mirror Falls. As she followed the stream she looked up at the sky to find white clouds gathering in little clumps. She had only come out in her T-shirt and shorts and she felt with relief a cool breeze play on her skin. *Please, please let the weather break so that I can go down to the dam and bury Dawn's reed.* It became a chant, filling her head as she walked. *Let the weather break, let the weather break.*

She entered the little coppice where she'd seen Dawn and heard her music. Would she come again to comfort her? Kite peered in among the trees, her nerve endings prickling, every sense alert. Then she heard an enormous splash. She hid behind a tree, held her breath and watched and waited as a human head broke the surface of the water. Was this Dawn gliding across the lake towards her with smooth, even strokes? But she was too far away to see and the sun glinted off the surface, reflecting light in every direction, playing tricks with her eyes. Kite hid and watched as the graceful figure swam towards her now, through the darker shaded water, till she came into view. It was not Dawn but Agnes Landseer. Kite's heart sank as Agnes emerged seal-like in her black swimming costume, wading towards her and now dancing her way over the sharp little stones and slates. She was surprisingly fit-looking, with swimmer's shoulders and lean strong limbs.

Agnes looked up momentarily, peering into the woodland as if she sensed that someone was watching. Kite did not move a muscle, and she held her breath steady so that she would not have to come face to face with her. Agnes wrapped a towel around her head, ducked behind a boulder and emerged dressed in a fleece and trousers. Kite shivered. It was cooler in the woodland, without the sun on her back. She scrunched her eyes closed as Agnes walked between the trees, treading only a few paces from where she hid. High above her head came the hollow tapping of a woodpecker. Agnes stopped in her tracks and peered up among the branches. Kite clung on to the trunk of the tree. When she was sure that Agnes was gone she stood up slowly and walked towards the lake. Behind her the woodpecker began its insistent tap-tapping again as if it was calling her back into the shelter of the wood.

Kite looked up to where the red birds circled above her head. She followed a path past the waterfall where she had stood with Garth and around the edge of the lake. At the far end was a high rock platform. Above it the hillside receded and the branches of a large tree hung out over the water. From one of these sturdy branches a thick rope swing had been securely tied. Kite clambered up. Maybe if she flew through the air like a bird Dawn would come and sit by her side just once more. It was so long since she'd been on the trapeze she wondered if her muscles would be strong enough to hold her. Then again, what harm could it do? The worst that could happen is that she'd fall into the lake and have to swim to the edge as Agnes had done. She climbed up on to another step-like ledge and finally pulled herself on to a piece of rock that jutted out over the lake like a diving board. Kite tugged on the rope to check that it was firm and attempted to climb up as she'd so often done in training with Annalisa. She pulled herself towards the tree, her arms shaking with the effort. It was hard to believe how weak she had become.

'Come on, Kite,' she willed herself on and climbed to the top then down again on to the slate platform. She wrapped the ends of the rope around her leg so that it was secure, returned to the back of the platform and began to run towards the lake. As she did, the kites above her sent up a deafening screech. She stretched backwards and let her body glide over the lake, she felt the breeze in her hair and the moment of forgetting that always came with flying . . . then she opened her eyes as she flew and looked down into the deep clear water. There was Dawn smiling up at her.

The water was ice cold, and as she hit the surface her heart clamped in shock as her body sank down, down, down to the bottom of the lake, following the golden path of Dawn's smile. The water was surprisingly clear except for the bubbles rising from her own mouth as she slowly breathed the air out of her lungs, but as she drifted further and further away Dawn's face faded and Grandma Grace's voice surged through her body.

You know you have all my love, and no matter how far I am, or what trouble life brings, I will always be with you in spirit.

*

What was she doing here, putting her own life at risk? As she kicked her arms and legs to swim up to the surface her St Christopher released itself from around her neck. She cast about for it frantically, stirring up the mud on the lake bed and clouding the water. Her lungs felt as if they were about to explode and she knew if she left it any longer that she would not have the strength to return to the surface. It was then she felt the necklace being placed into her palm and her fist close tight around it. An arm wrapped around her waist and something pushed her upward with superhuman force, propelling her from the bottom of the lake up through millions of bubbles up, up, up through the clear water until she broke the surface. Kite opened her mouth and gulped the air into her starving lungs and began to cough and splutter violently. She caught sight of Bardsey swimming ahead of her, looking back in concern every few seconds and barking insistently. The hand moved from around her waist to under her chin and someone was pulling her now exactly as she and Dawn had practised together in life-saving lessons. Kite struggled against the helping hand as she began to kick her arms and legs. She closed her eyes for a second, preparing herself to find Dawn swimming by her side.

'Kite, are you OK?' It was Garth, hovering too close, ready to catch her as if he thought she might drown.

All Dammed Up Inside

'I got cramp from the cold, and my leg went a bit dead for a minute, that's all,' Kite explained as Garth wrapped a towel around her shoulders.

'I was coming for a swim anyway!' Garth said. 'But Bardsey here made such a fuss that I ended up sprinting down to the lake. Wait till I tell Gran that she's got a life-saving dog on her hands!' Garth laughed as Bardsey shook his drenched coat, showering them both with water.

'Catches folk out how cold it is to swim in the tarns. Maybe wasn't such a clever idea with a bang to your head like that either.' He pointed to the now purple bruise on her forehead. 'Hey, you're shivering.' He took the towel and started rubbing her arms and back. 'You need more layers,' he said, running over to his rucksack and pulling out a fleece. Kite attempted to pull her T-shirt away from where it clung to the contours of her body before he ran back to her.

'Here, take these too. They'll be way too big for

you, but they've got a drawstring waist! I always pack something in case the weather turns.' He handed her some jogging bottoms, indicating the boulder behind which Agnes had got dressed.

'Do you think the weather is going to change?' Kite asked him as she pulled on the clothes and attempted to stop her teeth from chattering.

Garth looked up at the kites flying above his head and listened to their incessant screeching.

'They're always noisier when the weather's on the turn.'

Kite closed her eyes and drew in a deep breath. Soon she would be able to give Dawn the burial she deserved and then she might be able to stop searching for her.

Garth skimmed stones while she dressed. She got the impression that he didn't believe her about the cramp, that he was waiting for her to tell him the truth.

'I saw your gran swimming here earlier,' Kite said as she came to stand by his side.

'She swims pretty much every day, rain or shine. She's even been known to break the ice!' Garth laughed as he skimmed a stone across the water. 'She loves this place, reckons it's full of "presences" though.'

'Do *you* believe in that sort of thing?' Kite asked.

Garth paused a moment before he spoke. 'Can't say

for sure, but what I will say is there are certain spots that give you a feeling of something else, something beyond what we can see.'

There was the determined little hammering of the woodpecker again, working away at the tree.

Kite agreed. Even without her visions of Dawn, there was no denying that this place had a charged atmosphere.

As Garth packed his rucksack he took out a newspaper wrapping she recognized, dipped his towel in the water, wrung it out and wrapped it around Jack's trout. 'That should keep it cool.'

'Where did you get that?' Kite asked.

'Your dad brought it over. He's fair cut up about old Jack going, isn't he? Gran will be too. Still, I'll cook this up and take the bones back to the sculpture as your dad wanted.' Garth sighed deeply. 'I dread giving Gran the news.'

'I thought they didn't like each other, Jack and her?'

'Not sure what's gone on between them . . . exactly. All I know is Gran got it into her head that Mirror Falls wasn't a good place for her, because the owls kept crashing into the windows.' Garth paused for a minute. 'Whatever it was they fell out about, it had something to do with that place. They'd been great friends before, but they never spoke again after it was built.'

The kites let out a screech. Garth lay back on the

mossy ground, crossed his arms behind his head and stared up at them. Kite lay down beside him, both now looking up at the sky where the great birds circled, their wings casting shadows on the lake below.

'What are they looking for?' asked Kite.

'I suppose they're just staking out their territory, protecting their nests.'

'Is that what you're doing with your sculpture?'

'Not sure, but now you put it like that . . . !'

'I wish it would rain soon.'

Garth turned to her in surprise and laughed. 'Most folk want it to be sunny forever, but I know what you mean. I could do with a change myself. Anyway, as soon as the reservoir starts to fill, my sheep's going under so that'll be the end of that one! I could do with starting something fresh anyway.'

It was not until they were high up on the path, surrounded by bracken, that Garth explained that they were walking the 'Corpse Road' where once the dead had been carried over the hills to the nearest graveyard.

'Why is everything about this place so full of death?' Kite sighed.

She could feel Garth's piercing stare as she looked out over the sunlit fell.

'Life and death all wrapped up together,' he said. 'Jack must have known these fells like the lines on his own face.'

Little wisps of clouds were crossing the sky like a flotilla of ghost ships.

As they walked Garth pointed out patches of yellow and blue flowers that clung on inside the crevices; some of them he told her had been around since the Ice Age. 'Delicate-looking things, but tough as rock,' he smiled, picking off a tiny blue star-shaped head and placing it in Kite's hand. Is that how he saw her? Delicate but tough? That's how she'd felt before Dawn . . . and maybe that's how she would feel again one day.

'Dawn's favourite flowers are bluebells!' Kite told him.

'Who's Dawn?'

Of course she had never once talked of Dawn to him, and there was no reason anyone else would have either.

'My best friend.'

She didn't know how or why it was so much easier to talk to this quietly spoken boy of sparse words than to any of her family or friends, or Miss Choulty, or Dr Sherpa. But as they walked in the sunshine, it seemed natural for her to tell him about Dawn. Maybe it was because he wasn't connected to anyone who had ever known her. Or perhaps it was because he didn't try to force her to talk. As she finally released the words she felt strangely numb, as if she was telling someone else's story.

Garth listened as she retraced her steps backwards to the Falling Day. He did not say much, except to acknowledge her words with the occasional nod or glance her way. At one point, when she felt she'd said all there was to say, he took her hand in his and they'd walked on in silence.

'You talk about her like she's still here with you,' he said after a long pause, and the words had started to flow again. Now she told him about the Dawn owl at Mirror Falls; seeing her image in a rock pool and in Kite Carrec; Dawn's music that seemed to flow in and out of her; and finally, her idea to bury Dawn's reed in the sheep sculpture to lay her spirit to rest.

'That would be a fair place to settle,' was all he said as they stepped across a narrow part of a stream, where a bank of tiny stones blocked the path of the water.

'That's exactly how I feel, as if I've been dammed up,' Kite explained.

'It's good you're talking now,' Garth said as they sat down by the stream.

Garth picked one stone off the little dam and held his hand out to Kite as if to say, *your turn*.

They removed a stone each until the tiniest ripple of water began to flow between the remaining stones.

'Sounds to me like it was your friend who was all dammed up inside.' Garth stood up again and offered her his hand once more as they crossed the stream. 'Dawn was why you'd been crying when I first met you.'

Kite nodded. 'Crying in my sleep. I don't seem to have any tears for her when I'm awake.'

'It looked like you'd been crying for a long time,' Garth commented.

'Is that why you were staring at me?'

'Partly . . .' He smiled, looking into Kite's eyes.

They walked on in silence for a while. It was as if her telling him about Dawn had sealed something between them. Later she found herself talking about her love of running and Annalisa and Circus Space and how it had always been her dream to fly on the cloud swing.

'I'd like to see you do that one day,' he said.

Kite wondered how it was possible to feel this at ease with someone you hardly knew.

'Recognize this place?' Garth asked. He had brought her over the fell and they now stood at the bottom of the track that led up to Mirror Falls. Kite had no idea how they had found their way back.

As Garth walked her up the track she realized that she had spent all day talking about Dawn, and he'd walked beside her and listened, not even interrupting with questions. But now she thought about it, what did she actually know about him?

'Where are your mum and dad?'

'I live with my mam, just up the coast. My dad went off to New Zealand,' Garth explained.

'What's he doing there?'

'Married again.' Garth shrugged as if it didn't bother him. 'He's got a new family now. It happened ages ago.'

Kite turned to Garth and was surprised to see tears welling in his eyes. As she placed a hand on his arm, the knot inside her unravelled a little more and she felt the emotion rise up in her.

'I'm sorry!' Garth apologized as he turned back towards her, no sign of tears now. 'I don't know what's got into me. I think it's with you talking about how much you miss your friend. It made me think – at least I *could* see my dad, if I wanted.'

'And you *do* want to?' Kite asked gently.

Garth nodded. 'I didn't think I was that bothered, till now.'

Out of all the things that people had said to her, it seemed to her that Garth alone had truly understood why she felt so wretched. There could be no going back to how Dawn and she had once been, no making amends and no reunions.

Kite Tails

When she arrived back at Mirror Falls Seth was full of talk about Garth's sculpture. He'd been amazed to find it nearly finished when he'd gone down to the dam.

'He had all these Brummie kids working on it too, said they were from this outward-bound centre. Did he tell you he's got a job there after the summer?'

Kite shook her head. It seemed there was a lot about Garth that she didn't know. Her hand still felt warm from where he had held her so caringly.

Seth seemed to have a hundred questions as he placed a bowl of soup in front of her.

'Whose clothes are those anyway?' he asked, suddenly noticing her oversized fleece and jogging bottoms.

'They're Garth's. We went for a swim.' Kite shrugged. 'The tarn's icy cold . . . Sorry, Seth,' she sighed pushing away her bowl. 'I'm not hungry and I can't talk now. I'm tired out.'

*

In the bathroom she looked at herself in the mirror. She felt different, her thoughts less tangled than they'd been in ages. She washed her hands and face with the soap that Seth had brought for himself. She had no wish to summon Dawn's scent now; no need because she sensed that the time was coming closer when she could bury the reed and bring Dawn peace.

Kite took the reed from the case, pouring a little water into the empty soap dish and soaking it, as she'd watched Dawn do so many times.

'Is this a present?' the woman with the thick bifocals asked her as she handed over the reed box.

Kite glanced up at Dawn, who was examining reeds on the other side of the shop.

'Yes, a birthday present for my friend over there,' Kite whispered.

'In that case . . . !' The woman winked, her twinkling eyes magnified behind her glasses, and placed the little box snugly in a velvet navy-blue drawstring pouch. 'She'll treasure this forever.'

Back in her room, Kite tucked the little case back inside the folds of her pillow, then gazed at the long tails of her birthday kite, floating across the room as if beckoning to her, the tiny triangles of colour wafting this way and that. She walked over to the open window and listened. There was the roar of the waterfall that had become such a constant she hardly heard it any more, but there was another sound too. She closed her eyes and listened as the wind began to swirl around her head. She crept over to the staircase and took two steps down. There was the Dawn owl imprinted on the window as clearly as ever, but through the glass the valley below seemed to be stirring. The trees bent on the breeze, stretching from side to side like dancers warming up.

Seth sensed her behind him as he lay on the sofa.

'Looks like the weather's finally changing,' he murmured.

She stared out at the darkening sky and watched the high clouds race across streaks of midnight blue. Strange how the sea and the sky can look so alike sometimes, thought Kite, as the moon appeared again from behind a dark cloud.

The kite tails wafted across her face, the bright colours seeping into her like paint as they tickled her skin. She opened her eyes and began to read her birthday messages. A sudden gust of wind pulled the whole kite off the wall and now it was dancing around the room in front of her, as if taunting her with its acrobatic skill. Kite jumped off the bed and went to grab hold of it, but it dodged her grasp and zigzagged down the driftwood staircase. Then it surged upward. Kite's hair lifted from her head and trailed behind her as if it too was a kite tail. She grabbed hold of the ends and tugged with all her might but the kite seemed to double in power. She looked down at her feet and felt the distance grow between the ground and her body; she looked up to see her kite glide out of the roof. Her breath flew with it as she was lifted higher and higher into the sky, bobbing gently on streams of air . . .

Kite kept her eyes closed, unwilling to be wrenched from her dream despite the force of the wind buffeting the house. Just for a second on waking she had felt the same sense of joy she'd experienced the day she'd first watched Annalisa fly, the same soaring feeling that came over her every time she'd been on the trapeze since.

On opening her eyes she half expected her kite to have flown away, but there it was, still tethered to the wall, although the tail had wafted across the room and wrapped itself around her bed like bunting.

As Kite padded down the driftwood staircase she noticed that the window was speckled with tiny droplets of water. One of the Dawn owl wings was beginning to fade. She'd imagined that a huge torrential rain would come in the night and clean the print away in one go, but she saw now how it would fade in time, gently, bit by bit.

Seth spent the morning composing. Kite recognized one song from a tune that Jack had sung, but he was also working on something new. It was always a painful stop-start process listening to him compose.

Usually the melody came easily to him but the words were always more difficult.

> '*We walked among the gravestones in the sunniest of*
> *ways*
> *Now the sky's troubled by a hundred coloured greys*
> *It all must come to an end one day and when it does*
> *the very least you should say*
> *Is the road has been long and winding*
> *Yes! The road should be long and winding.*'

Kite heard a break in Seth's voice as he sang the last words. 'The road *should* be long and winding.'

When he'd finished he came to find her. She had set the table for them both and made a black coffee for Seth and a plate full of pancakes. She'd realized as she let the butter sizzle in the pan that this unfamiliar feeling rumbling inside her was hunger.

'Something smells good.' Seth sniffed the air as he came to join her in the kitchen. He kissed her on the head and sat down. 'So come on then, spill the beans. What's he like, this Garth?'

'He doesn't say much,' Kite answered.

'Neither do you, lately,' Seth said with a sigh, reaching over the table and ruffling her hair.

Kite gently pushed him away.

'What! I can't mess up your hair now!'

'He's invited me for lunch.' Kite sprinkled sugar

on her pancake. Seth watched her intently as she ate. She wished he wouldn't be so set on trying to read her mood.

'You go then! I said I'd help out with the funeral arrangements today.'

Seth set off mid-morning. 'What time's Garth coming to fetch you?' He asked as he left.

'In about an hour,' Kite answered.

Seth nodded and lingered in the doorway. 'Tell him to walk you back here by five o'clock.'

Kite nodded. She would have liked to take her hand and smooth away the worry wrinkles on his forehead. 'I told Garth about Dawn and I think it's helped,' she found herself saying instead.

Seth paused and for a moment she thought she saw a hurt look cross his face. Then his mouth twisted into a smile of relief. 'That's good, my love.'

Kite watched him walk away from her towards the car.

'Seth!' she called out to him, and heard how sharp and urgent her voice had suddenly become.

'What is it?'

'I like the new song.'

'I wrote it for Dawn,' he said, then gently closed the door behind him.

Clearing

What was the matter with her? She had hardly thought about her appearance since she'd got here. From what she already knew about Garth, he wasn't the sort of person who would care what she wore anyway. She looked around the room at the rejected clothes strewn everywhere. Her leggings were too clingy, her denim shorts too brief, even though he'd seen her wearing practically nothing the day before. She couldn't wear her skirt because they would probably go walking. In the end she'd gone for a combination of layered-up long- and short-sleeved T-shirts and an old baggy jumper of Seth's that she'd cut over the shoulder. She pulled on her skinny jeans and laced up her navy DMs. She looked at herself in the bathroom mirror. She had definitely lost weight and muscle; even under all these layers she looked and felt smaller than she had before.

Kite sat at the kitchen table and waited. When she heard Bardsey bark on the path below she had

241

to resist the temptation to run over to the glass stepping stones to greet them. Now here were Garth and Bardsey standing behind the glass entrance. Kite thought Garth looked different, more like he had on the day she'd bumped into him outside the Carrec Arms. He was wearing a thick navy blue jumper, a padded jacket and jeans.

As Kite released the door Bardsey pushed past her and ran through to the living room. By the time Garth and Kite had caught up with him he was comfortably lounging on the sofa admiring the view.

'You cheeky lad.' Garth laughed, patting his head and looking up at the window.

'So this is the owl print.'

Kite nodded as Garth walked over and studied the fading markings of the wingspan.

'It's a work of nature. I wish I could paint something as beautiful as that.' Garth was staring at Kite now.

'Do you paint too then?' she asked.

'I try. I did the landscape on this blind here.' Garth pointed up to where it was folded into the glass cavity.

'That was you?'

Garth nodded. 'Come on, Bardsey. Let's be off. Gran's waiting for us.'

'The wind's really getting up now.' Garth surveyed the sky. 'Come on. I'll take you on my favourite woodland path.'

As they walked together through the woods, the trees swaying above their heads, branches bending low, she wished that he would hold her hand again. The wind splayed her hair all over her face and she had to part it like a veil to see where she was going. A red squirrel darted up a tree to their right, its bushy tail appearing and disappearing as it helter-skeltered around and around.

'I've never seen a red squirrel before!'

'Really? There's loads around here.'

As they walked deeper into the wood Kite couldn't help remembering how in nursery Dawn had hated all those Grimms' fairy tales of children getting lost in the woods, while *she* had loved them. Even when they were very small Dawn had been afraid of so many things that had never bothered Kite. But Kite had come to realize as they'd grown older that what Dawn had feared more than anything else was failure. She had played so beautifully in so many concerts. Why had it hit her so hard when once, just once, things didn't go according to plan? It wouldn't have mattered to Dawn what Esme said – that a reed failed every player at some point in their career; Dawn would not have heard that. And why did it have to happen so close to exams too, when Dawn was already winding herself up into an A* frenzy?

Garth grabbed a stick and started slashing back branches as the woodland became denser.

'You do know your way through, don't you?' Kite asked.

'Shhh . . . !' Garth whispered, placing a hand on Bardsey's head to still him. The dog sniffed the air expectantly.

Ahead, a small clearing was lit by a shaft of sunlight streaking through the dense leaf canopy. A single red deer appeared from behind a tree like a mythical creature bathed in sunshine. They watched spellbound as it foraged among the fallen leaves. The branch above Kite creaked and the deer lifted its head, ears pricked, and stared in their direction. Kite held her breath as it sought them out, tracing their presence between the trees, its legs quivering like those of a sprinter preparing to bolt. Garth looked at Kite and smiled. She smiled back, her heart thudding drum-like in her chest. As they gazed at each other it was as if she'd taken the remote and switched off the sound to everything but the deafening chamber of her own breath.

To her left a red tail flashed across her field of vision as the squirrel continued its spiral journey further up the tree. Bardsey began to bark at it, and when Kite looked back at the clearing, the deer had fled.

'Bonny, wasn't she?' Garth said, still looking straight at Kite.

The words of Jack's song played through her head as she stepped into the clearing.

'When you look around here you see trees of all ages and sizes,' said Garth, following her into the glade. 'The little ones with bright new leaves, so spindly they can whip over in the wind, then middling trees, just getting on with the seasons, growing each year, and finally, the great hearts of the forest. That's what I call the really ancient ones. You can feel the strength in them.'

This was the most Kite had ever heard him say in one go. The way he spoke reminded her of something Dawn had said: 'Never mistake a quiet mouth for a quiet mind.' And here was the proof.

Garth cleared away the leaves from a hollowed-out trunk of a tree. It had been smoothed and sanded into a chair shape.

'Another one of your sculptures?'

He nodded. 'I've been coming here every summer since Dad left! I think at first Gran had me over because she felt guilty about Dad going. Anyway, I've been hanging around here for long enough to have a few bits and pieces scattered around the place.'

'But no one's ever going to see this!' Kite cleared away more leaves and sat down.

'I'm not fussed.' Garth shrugged. 'I made it for my dad, but he hasn't been back here to see it yet.' Despite his efforts to hide it, she could read the unhappiness in his eyes. It must have taken him hours to carve this out. Kite knew plenty of people at school whose parents had split up, but most of them saw both of their parents all the time.

'When did your dad leave?'

'I was eleven, just before secondary school.'

'And you haven't seen him since?'

Garth shook his head and smoothed his hands over the seat. 'I'd better warn you,' he said suddenly. 'My gran gets kind of low from time to time.'

Kite had not expected him to change the subject so quickly. Garth had taken a stick and was poking the leaves, stirring the earth as he spoke.

'Gran's fine most of the time,' Garth was saying now. 'Dr Sherpa's been grand with her, but sometimes it's like she takes a tumble in here –' Garth tapped the side of his head – 'and then she's in a very dark spot. Mam's coming over to pick her up later. She's always refused to come to us before, but this time she's agreed it's for the best, just for a while. Mam's going to teach her to drive at the same time as me, she says, so she'll not be so shut off out here when winter sets in.'

Kite nodded, suddenly feeling shaken by the idea of Garth leaving too.

'But you're staying, aren't you?'

'Aye!' Garth smiled at her. 'We've still got to go down to the dam with Dawn's reed, haven't we?'

Kite smiled back. She would have liked to have hugged him to thank him for remembering, but there was an awkwardness between them today that she hadn't felt before. She watched as he turned over a fallen branch with a stick and hundreds of tiny woodlice scrambled out into the light. Kite stared at the panicking insects as they skittered around desperately in search of a dark earthy place to hide. Garth turned the branch back over and the woodlice scampered to safety.

'As soon as I told Gran about Jack I knew something was coming. Last night she had one of her turns, got all confused and went sleepwalking into the barn. I found her sitting crying in the straw loft saying how she'd spoilt everything.'

'Maybe I shouldn't come over, if she's not well.'

'She'll be even more disappointed if you don't. She's spent all morning baking for you.'

For the first time Kite had a clear view of a tiny stone cottage nestled into the side of the hill. Beside it was an ancient barn. The wind formed a tunnel through this narrow part of the valley and the buildings were exposed to its vicious blast. Kite wondered if this was the kind of place where her great-grandparents, whoever they were, might once have lived. Enclosed behind a drystone wall was a wild-flower garden with well-tended raised beds. Tomatoes, strawberries, Canterbury bells, tall pokers of foxgloves and lupins all jostled for space with white roses that scrambled over the whitewashed walls. The whole garden swayed as flower heads dislodged themselves, flew through the air and finally settled on the ground like confetti. The tiny blue door was open and bashed noisily against its post. Bardsey barked and sprang ahead of them as he spied Agnes, her grey hair flying in the wind. She was cradling something in her arms like a baby.

Scar View

As they drew close Agnes set down the bleating lamb, and it skitted towards the garden. Bardsey ran over and guided it back inside as Garth quickly closed the door against the force of the wind. Once the lamb was safe inside Bardsey sat beside it and nuzzled its curly coat; it nosed him back and settled down, its skinny body pushed up close against the collie's side.

'You're supposed to round them up, not mother them!' Garth laughed at Bardsey as he stroked his head fondly.

Kite bent down and touched the soft woolly head of the lamb. Its coat was surprisingly coarse and oily and smelt of sweet milk. Agnes returned to her seat by an old-fashioned range and began feeding another lamb from a bottle. It tugged strongly on the teat, its little tail knocking against the table in excitement. Kite was struck by the gentle expression on Agnes's face. Dr Sherpa was right – someone who was so kind to animals, and who obviously loved her dog and her grandson so much, could not be all bad. After its last greedy glugs, the lamb leaped off her lap and scampered sideways on its skinny legs, abruptly crash-landing on top of Bardsey's back. He shook it off, like he would a naughty pup, and licked its face.

'Daft things, they are, all of them!' Garth smiled. 'We're not always such a menagerie. The farmer fetches Gran the orphans to bring on. These two are very late in the season.' He leaned down towards Agnes and placed a comforting hand on her shoulder. 'OK, Gran?'

She patted his arm reassuringly by way of answer. 'I hoped you'd come,' she said in Kite's direction.

Kite scanned the low room with its stone floor and old pine table. A kettle was steaming on the stove and the place smelt of warm cake and yeasty bread. Garth gestured for Kite to sit down as he walked through to a well-stocked pantry. Two large buckets of water stood on the floor and glass jars of pickles, jams and honey filled the shelves. From the far wall hung a collection of large hessian sacks of the kind that Kite had seen Agnes carrying. Garth returned with a jug of apple juice and three mugs.

'You thirsty, Gran?'

She shook her head. There was something listless about her today and she was hardly recognizable as the woman Kite had watched swimming in the tarn.

Kite saw in her lifeless expression a reflection of the same numb feeling that had settled somewhere deep inside her on the Falling Day.

'You got my thank-you note?' Agnes was asking. Her voice had flattened out into a tuneless monotone.

Kite nodded in reply as her mind whirred with questions about Mirror Falls, and yet at the same time she felt an urgent need to escape the tiny room that seemed to be crammed full of Agnes's pain.

'Mind if I use the bathroom?'

'We're not on the mains here,' Garth explained, 'but we've got the throne outside!'

As she surveyed the room she noticed that it was full of oil lamps. There was not even a switch on the wall.

Kite followed Garth through the garden and along the side of the cottage.

'You wouldn't credit it, would you, but Mam says a journalist once called Gran "the most ambitious woman in Britain". I wonder what they'd make of her outside loo!'

When they got back to the cottage Agnes was nowhere to be seen. A loaf of warm bread and a tray of cheeses and boiled eggs with curiously mottled grey-green shells had been placed on the table along with a whole lettuce glinting with water droplets. Cherry tomatoes and strawberries were piled up in crude earthenware pots. Kite picked up an egg and turned it over in her hands.

Garth leaned his head out of the window, and yelled at the top of his voice, 'Thanks, Gran!'

Kite looked towards the garden, to see Agnes walking off holding her driftwood crook, the lambs skittering along beside her.

'Tuck in!' Garth broke off a great wedge of bread and offered a chunk to Kite.

The butter melted straight in. Kite's stomach rumbled so loudly that it sounded like a whine. Bardsey, who was sitting under the table, looked up and whined back, which set Garth and Kite off laughing.

'That's the first time I've heard you really laugh,' he said.

Immediately Kite felt overtaken by a now-familiar stab of guilt, for feeling happy even for a second. She stood up from the table and went over to the window.

'Does she run this whole place herself?'

'I help out in the holidays, chop wood and set her straight for winter, but, aye, she's here on her own mostly. I think that's why she comes across a bit . . . well, let's just say she keeps her own company these days. I had an idea to give her Bardsey here –' Garth broke off a piece of bread and fed it to the dog – 'to remind her that she's got family not so very far away. He's named Bardsey after the place I'm from, just down the coast.'

Kite watched Agnes wander through the garden cutting long-stemmed flowers. She couldn't help thinking how strange it was that someone who had built houses out of glass could be so impossible to see into.

Kite recognized the sound of the Land Rover straight away.

'That'll be Doctor Sherpa and my mam, come to sort Gran out ready to take her back to our house,' Garth said, jumping up.

A white van drew up behind Dr Sherpa. Garth walked down the path, indicating for Kite to follow. He wrapped his arm around Agnes's shoulders as she waited by the gate. Then a tall woman with short brown hair opened the van door and Garth strode towards her with his arms outstretched.

'I've missed you, son,' Kite heard her say as she patted his shoulders.

Dr Sherpa looked up and waved at Kite and Agnes, who were now standing side by side. Agnes touched her arm gently.

'I would like to show you something, before I go,' she murmured.

Kite nodded but felt as if she would like to run away from Agnes's intense gaze. She looked small and vulnerable, and the image of the frightened deer drifted into Kite's mind.

'Didn't expect to see you here, Kite! How about this for a change in temperature?' Dr Sherpa chatted on. 'Now don't go catching a chill,' he warned, ushering Agnes back into the cottage. Bardsey was in a frenzy of excitement, running backwards and forward between Garth and Kite. Kite knelt down and patted him.

'Mam, this is Kite!'

'Hi! I'm Libby! I'll be through in a minute,' she called as she propped open the doors of the van with a garden spade and fork. She was dressed for hard work in her wellies, jeans and thick fisherman's jumper. Garth didn't look much like her, but then he'd already said that he looked more like his dad and Agnes's side of the family.

Agnes was now sitting by the stove, Bardsey settled faithfully by her side. Dr Sherpa pulled a chair up beside her and took her hands in his. Kite was surprised how at ease the two of them seemed together, as if they were old friends rather than doctor and patient.

Garth poured tea from a large green enamel pot, placed a scone on a saucer and handed it to the doctor.

'Agnes, you spoil me and it's starting to show!' he patted his protruding stomach. 'But thank you.'

'It's nothing! Call it the last tea!' Agnes sighed as

she watched Libby carrying two small suitcases into the van.

'Come on, Agnes!' Dr Sherpa, coaxed. 'There'll be plenty more teas. You get yourself driving before the winter and I can return the compliment. I'll cook you a curry myself!'

'Is that a promise?'

Dr Sherpa nodded. 'Now I've spoken to Libby's doctor and he's signed you up as a temporary patient, we're all in order.'

Agnes looked tentatively over to Kite. 'I just want to show Kite the barn.'

There was something in Dr Sherpa's expression that seemed to be asking Kite to do him a favour. 'OK, I'll help Libby and Garth with the packing then,' he said. 'Don't be too long. You'll want to be on your way, Agnes, before the weather rolls in.'

Agnes stood and walked over to the table where Kite was sitting.

'Shall we go and see then?'

Curtain of Cobwebs

Agnes led the way down the pebble path, through the gate and out towards the barn. As she opened the enormous solid wooden door she stumbled backwards and Kite placed a steadying hand on her back. The wind streamed in, wafting hay and straw into a dust storm. It took all of Kite's strength to push the great door closed behind them.

The only light in the barn came through tiny slits cut into the stone high above their heads. Kite gleaned nothing unremarkable as flecks of straw and dust settled and the lambs bleated a greeting. Agnes walked towards the far end of the barn. Kite followed close behind, her eyes adjusting to the gloom. A few sweet-smelling hay bales were loaded on top of each other and some rusted farming implements hung from the walls along with the familiar hessian sacks. A bottle-green tractor was parked up, the same one that Kite had seen Garth driving on their way up to Mirror Falls on the first day. Above her head the ancient oak rafters were strung with giant cobwebs and lit by streams of white light. Without speaking, Agnes began to climb the ancient loft ladder, beckoning Kite to follow. On the upper level lay a thick bed of straw. Agnes walked over to a hard egg-shaped object about the size of a cricket ball and picked it up off the ground.

'Owl pellet,' she said quietly, examining it.

Kite felt a fluttering of fear and excitement rise up in her as she inspected the mangled ball. She had read about these pellets in the *Owl Lore* book. They were what the owl regurgitated after it had digested all the goodness from its food. There was something gross and fascinating about them at the same time.

'Want to see what's inside?' Agnes didn't wait for a reply but picked up a stick and started to break up the matted ball. Between the indistinguishable mush of digested material there were tiny bones and feathers and the skull of either a mouse or vole. It reminded Kite a bit of Garth's sculpture, the way all the natural elements were meshed together.

'How are you now?' Agnes asked suddenly. 'I've been thinking about you since the day we met on the road.'

'Why?' whispered Kite.

'I sensed your sadness.'

Kite's heart was thudding hard. She would have liked to retreat down the ladder right now, but she felt

257

that she had allowed herself to be drawn into Agnes's web and there was no escape.

'I know about your friend.'

Kite nodded slowly. She ought to feel angry with Garth and maybe even Dr Sherpa for talking to Agnes about Dawn, but instead she found herself waiting for some kind of explanation.

Out of the corner of her eye Kite saw something quiver. Agnes followed her gaze. She placed her fingers to her lips and stood up slowly, gesturing for Kite to follow as she tiptoed over to where the oak rafters converged. The ancient beams seemed to be decorated here by an ornate curtain of cobwebs. Kite peered through the veil of filigree threads to where she could just make out the sturdy curved back of an owl.

'She's why I left you that note.' Agnes nodded in the owl's direction.

'The Dawn owl!' Kite whispered. 'So she's still alive.'

'This is the owl that flew at your window. I've been looking after her, but she's fine now. The vet says there's nothing wrong with her except maybe she's becoming tame,' Agnes whispered as they both stared at her ghostly form. 'She's only young. I expect she'll find a mate soon. They mate for life, you know.' Agnes fell silent as if her mind had momentarily wandered.

Kite let herself sink down into the straw. Was she dreaming this?

'But there's something important I want to say. Garth thinks it might help you to understand about your friend.' Agnes kneeled down next to Kite. 'I started feeling low when I was about thirteen years old and it's been on and off all through my life,' Agnes stared at the owl as she spoke. It was almost dark now inside the barn and the fact that Kite could hardly see Agnes made it easier to listen to her talk so frankly. It felt like a confessional.

'I was lucky – I managed to struggle on through the milestones: school, college, university, but there were moments when I thought I wouldn't make it. I think people let me off with being a bit distant from time to time because I was one of those gifted types. I was getting architecture commissions in cities all over the place; on paper, at least, everyone thought my life was perfect!'

'People thought Dawn was perfect . . . That's what they wrote about her in the papers – they called her "The Perfect Dawn"!'

Agnes nodded. 'Sometimes it felt like . . .' Agnes's voice petered out and she took a deep breath to compose herself. 'Well, sometimes it felt like it would be easier to stop than to fail, but I managed to keep going and then David came along, Garth's dad, and I wasn't expecting him, but anyway he was a blessing because after that I lived for him. Him and my work of course, always my work.'

'I didn't know . . . I didn't even guess that Dawn was feeling so low . . .'

'That's why Garth asked me to talk to you. He told me that you might think it was somehow your fault, and that's the thing I know that your friend would never ever want you to feel.'

Kite was shaking now. Agnes placed an arm around her shoulders and held her close, and Kite began to feel as if she was talking to this strange woman for a reason. 'Your friend didn't give herself or you or anyone else the chance to help her. It's tragic for her and her poor family . . . and heartbreaking for you, her best friend –' Agnes sighed – 'but it's not your fault, and she would want you to know that too; you can't go on feeling guilty for being alive. You've got to go forward with your life and find some happiness for yourself.'

Over Agnes's shoulder Kite watched as the owl's head swivelled to face her through the veil of cobwebs.

'The way owls look at you, it's like they're searching out the truth. Don't you think?' Agnes paused.

'When I saw her smash into Mirror Falls I thought she had Dawn's face.'

'Maybe that was the truth for you then, but what do you see now?' Agnes asked.

'Just an owl,' Kite whispered.

Agnes nodded. 'There are so many ways of finding happiness. I only wish I'd realized that when I was younger.'

From the owl's throat came a gentle contented gurgling sound. She hopped closer now, pushing through the cobweb curtain. Here she was with her creamy-white feathers and golden-brown markings within touching distance. The owl slow-blinked at her, as if in recognition.

'Let's leave her in peace,' Agnes whispered, and began to feel her way back down the ladder.

The lambs bleated noisily and their little tails knocked furiously against the stone wall. Agnes opened the pen gate, holding it for Kite, and they walked in. Agnes knelt down and lifted a lamb under each arm and handed one to Kite. It squirmed and wriggled, nuzzling into her, and started sucking on her finger. She was amazed how strong it was for such a skinny little thing. Kite laughed as it leaped out of her arms despite her desperate efforts to hang on to it.

'They'll be let back out on the fells soon, roaming around with Jack,' Agnes said. 'I can't tell you how I felt when Garth brought that trout home . . . like Jack was sending me a farewell message. You see he always used to catch a trout for me to cook for him.' They were both sitting together now in the gloom of the barn with the lambs nestling up to them. Kite felt sorry for Agnes; sitting this close to her she could feel her sadness too, and then she heard the old lady's sobs rising as she cradled the lamb closer to her and rocked back and forth. 'I loved him, you know.'

To Kite's relief she heard the barn door being pushed open.

'Everything all right, Gran?' Garth asked as he came over to them, looking from Agnes to Kite and back again. Kite shook her head. Garth opened the little gate and sat beside Agnes. She leaned her head on his shoulder, and through her tears she began to speak. She told them it was a story that no one else must ever know, a story that was meant to put things right, and that she was telling it to Garth and Kite because they were the next generation and had a chance of understanding what was important in life.

It was an odd gathering – Kite, Agnes with her lambs, and Garth – sitting together in the gloomy barn with the Dawn owl above as witness to Agnes's confession.

The Passing Bell

After Dr Sherpa dropped her off she went straight
upstairs and lay down. She slept heavily without
dreaming. It was as if she had reached a point of
overload and had to switch off from the world and
everything in it.

'Kite, I'm sorry to have to wake you . . .' Seth placed
a hand on her arm.

She scrunched her eyes closed, longing to sink back
into the comforting arms of this rare dreamless sleep.
She felt as she had once when she'd drifted off on the
beach in St Kitts and woken to feel the sun warming
her from the inside.

'I told Ellie you'd help her with the flowers!' Seth
sat down on the bed next to her.

She opened her eyes. Seth was already dressed for
the funeral, in a thin dark purple jumper, pale blue
shirt and black cotton trousers. She didn't feel like
going, but she could see how much it meant to him
and strangely, since Agnes's confession about Jack,

she felt she should go for her sake.

'OK! Give me a minute! What time is it anyway?'

'Early. Ellie says wild flowers wilt if you pick them the night before, so she's been out to get them this morning and she wants you to help her arrange them.'

'This must be hard, with your friend dying so recently,' Ellie said gently as they sat around the table tying posies.

'When did your parents die?' Kite asked.

Ellie looked up at Kite as if she was surprised that Kite remembered what she'd told her. 'I was fourteen when they had the accident,' she replied simply. 'It's always really been Grandad here for me since then.'

'It must have been awful for you too, the shock of it,' Kite whispered.

Ellie placed a little posy in Kite's hand, 'This is for you!' She smiled through eyes brim-full of tears. 'Because it's hard not to get the chance to say goodbye.'

Kite nodded, but as she concentrated on tying the bows, she felt stronger than she had in weeks. The slow blink of the Dawn owl, so accepting and full of understanding, kept returning to her and bringing with it calm.

Later, as they walked up to the church, Ellie explained to her and Seth the meaning of the Passing Bell.

'The first tolls will tell you if it's a fella or lass: don't

264

ask me why, but it's five for a fella, four for a lass, and –' Ellie placed a comforting arm around Kite's shoulders – 'three for a bairn. After that you get a toll for every year of your life . . . I always think how sweet it sounds that old tenor bell, for such a sad occasion.'

On the third toll a gust of wind lifted Kite's hair from her shoulders. She looked up at the greying sky as the clouds billowed across like smoke wafting from a chimney. Was this the wind that would signal rain at last?

'Three tolls for a bairn . . .' She heard Ellie's voice echoing through her head.

The bell rang out across the fell. On the sixteenth toll Kite's tears began to fall for how short a life Dawn had lived – they had only been standing around the grave for five minutes. That's all it would have taken if the Passing Bell had been rung out for Dawn. But today the bell rang on and on, marking each year of Jack's long life. On the thirtieth toll one of the mourners took what looked like an umbrella stick with a little piece of leather at the end, stuck it in the ground and rested his behind on it, like a little seat.

'He might have been faster, but I'll keep you all standing longer! Still, a fair old innings,' another old man muttered.

It was clear that several of the older people had been to many funerals and that this place was as familiar to them as the Carrec Arms.

Kite hardly heard the priest's words after the ninety-ninth toll had sounded.

Agnes's tearstained face entered Kite's mind again as she glanced over at Jack's wife's grave and Ellie dropped the first clods of earth on to the coffin.

Up until this point she had seemed calm and collected, but now her whole body shook in great racking sobs.

A dog barked a little way off up the fell. Kite turned to find Bardsey bounding up to greet her at the church wall. Garth whistled and he obediently ran back to his side. He was holding a bunch of flowers in his hands, the blooms Agnes had been collecting in her garden when the wind had blown the flower heads like confetti at the wedding that might have been between Jack and Agnes. If only she hadn't spoilt her chance of happiness by pursuing her obsession of building the perfect home. Garth had been as amazed as Kite to hear the story of how she had demolished the owl habitat where they had nested for generations, and fought with Jack and lost him because of it.

In the bouquet from Agnes's garden there were pale pink roses and foxgloves, impressive stems of lupins and delphiniums that she had grown and picked with her own hands.

Garth leaned over the wall and handed them to Kite.

'Agnes asked if you'd be kind enough to put these on Jack's grave.' She could feel his warm breath on her ear. 'I'll come to Mirror Falls tomorrow morning so we can do the rest of what Gran asked.'

Kite took the bouquet from him and glanced at Ellie, half expecting her to invite Garth back to the Carrec Arms, but she was already walking away. And when Kite turned back to see where Garth was he had already disappeared over the brow of the hill.

'She's got no business sending her showy flowers!' Ellie snapped as they slowly processed away from the church.

'Don't be too harsh on her, Ellie. She's hard enough on herself. And she's been very unwell these last few days,' Dr Sherpa counselled.

'All I know is that he had that stroke on the way back from Mirror Falls after begging her not to demolish the old barn. Then she did it anyway. The week before that he'd been as fit as a fiddle, running up to Kite Carrec and back. She probably put a hex on him, the old witch.' Ellie was sobbing again now and Dr Sherpa was attempting to calm her down as she grabbed the flowers off Kite, marched them back up to the grave and threw them on to the coffin.

'Seems like the owls got their own back and drove her out anyway.'

Kite wrapped her arms around herself and shivered. The temperature had dropped and the long grasses surrounding the churchyard swayed wildly in the quickening wind.

Jack's seat had been pushed up close to the table making it clear that it was *not* to be sat on. Over the back of the chair Ellie had placed his tweed jacket and cap.

'I think I'll light the fire for him. He always liked the hearth lit up,' Ellie said, busying herself.

Aida, a woman with a wave of hair sprayed purplish grey, manoeuvred herself into the pub in a large silver wheelchair with a little help over the step from Dr Sherpa. In her lap she had gathered a small bunch of forget-me-nots, the exact same blue as the sky had been for all the time that they'd been in the Lakes so far. Kite thought their centres looked like modest yellow suns.

'I heard the passing bell for Jack and just about managed to reach over my great girth for these!'

Ellie kissed Aida fondly on the cheek, took the flowers from her and arranged them in a tiny glass vase which she placed on the table in front of Jack's chair.

'Not that anyone around here's ever likely to forget him.' Aida smiled.

'He'll be at peace now with Joyce. She was always the love of his life.'

Kite thought of how Agnes had sobbed when she'd told them that the two of them had planned to marry when Mirror Falls was complete, and how nervous Jack had been about telling Ellie.

'You know,' cackled Aida, 'I asked Jack to wed me once, but he turned me down kindly, maybe for the best. It wouldn't have been decent being a widow three times over!' Then she seemed to freeze as she wheeled a little closer to Seth.

'For a minute, lad, I thought I was seeing ghosts!'

Aida looked to Ellie to introduce them.

'This is Seth. His grandmother was from around here. Grandad was helping him to trace her.'

'Shame he never thought to ask me! But then I suppose Jack would never have met him, though he knew all about Lily, of course!'

At the mention of Lily's name, Seth looked down at Aida.

'It is Lily you think you're related to? Am I right?'

Seth looked dumbfounded.

'Don't you think he's the spit of him, Giles?' Aida asked, turning to a tiny bald man wearing an old-fashioned waistcoat who stood nearby.

He took a pair of half-spectacles from his pocket and placed them on the end of his nose.

'Can't say. I only set eyes on the beggar once when I was home on leave.'

'So you know who I'm thinking of?' Aida raised her eyebrows questioningly.

'If I'd have got hold of him, he wouldn't have gone back to Germany in one piece,' butted in a tall man with a shock of white hair, wearing a dapper black suit and tie.

'Oh for pity's sake, Lance, can you never make your peace?'

Seth stared from Giles to Aida to Lance, a look of complete bewilderment on his face.

'Go on then. You tell them, Aida. I'm just amazed you've managed to keep it to yourself for all this time.' Giles grimaced, not exactly kindly.

'I've got plenty of secrets you'll never know about,' Aida retorted.

'I shouldn't wonder!'

Aida ignored him and turned back to Seth. 'You've got a look of your grandad, that's for sure –' she nodded at him – 'but this bonny lass is the picture of Lily. Jack must have seen that . . . Strange how the likeness finds its way out generations down, isn't it? They used to call Lily Storey the belle of the valley. She was as pretty as a primrose too –' she smiled at Kite – 'and the best friend I ever had.'

'I'm sorry, I don't understand.' Seth sat down on the bench next to Aida.

'The prisoners of war helped work the farms round here, while our lads were off fighting. Some of them were no more than young boys.' She glanced over to Seth. 'I remember Peter – he was a looker like you and sweet-natured with it. I never saw him complain even though he hardly had an hour off. But whenever he did, he used to make these toys for Lily. He gave one to me once too.'

'I bet he did,' mumbled Lance bad-temperedly.

Aida shot him a dirty look.

'I've still got it. You can have it if you want,' she continued. 'Peter Klein was his name, had the voice of an angel. He used to sing to us – we hadn't a clue what the words meant, but his voice could melt your heart. Lily was only sixteen and I think he was eighteen or nineteen. Then the war was over and he was packed back to Germany before anyone knew, and well . . . the shame of it, you know,' Aida sighed, pointing down at her own round belly.

'They said he forced hissel' on her,' Lance growled. His face was flushed with anger. Kite couldn't believe that something that had happened so long ago could still provoke such strong feeling.

'However it was . . . they packed the bairn off as soon as she was born. Lily named her though. I remember that because it was the name she gave her first doll when she was just five years old – she told me then that she was going to call her baby girl Hannah, and that's what she did when her time came.'

'That baby was my mum!' Seth whispered, as if he'd been winded. Kite had never seen him look so stunned, and she felt breathless and churned up herself.

'There's no doubt in my mind. It's like a piece of

Lily has come back to me after all this time.'

So Aida had known Lily since she was small too, just as Kite had met Dawn in nursery. It was touching to see how much she still missed her. I never want to forget Dawn either, Kite thought.

Seth stood up and started pacing around the table. He rummaged in his pocket for his rolling tobacco and walked out into the lane. As Kite followed him Aida placed a hand on her arm and pointed to the back of her wheelchair.

Outside they found Seth drawing heavily on his roll up.

Although there was no one else about, Aida lowered her voice to a whisper so that Seth and Kite both had to lean in to hear what she said next.

'I'm maybe the only person in these parts that can tell you this. Your grandma swore me to keep it to myself, but it seems to me you're supposed to know.'

Seth nodded and ground his butt into the road.

'It's not true what they said. He didn't force hissel' on her, though it made them feel better to think it. They were in love, and she begged them to let her keep the bairn, but . . . It breaks my heart still to remember her crying out for her little Hannah, long after she was gone.' Aida took one of Seth's hands and held it tight as if she hardly dared ask the question. 'Is your mam still with us?'

Seth shook his head sadly.

Aida's eyes filled with tears and soon Kite found herself welling up too. It seemed so wrong that her Grandma Hannah whom she'd never met had died thinking she was unwanted by her natural parents.

'I've no wish to upset you, lass –' Aida reached to wipe the tears from Kite's eyes – 'but it does you good to know that you come from love, no matter how old you get. Lily told me when they sent the lad away that she would never love again, and I can tell you she had plenty of offers.' She pointed into the pub and smiled with satisfaction. 'Do you know she turned them all down, the lot of them in there!'

Kite let the tears roll down her cheeks for the great-grandmother she had never known. Seth placed an arm around her shoulders and smiled at her through his own tears.

'Thanks for caring. Well, at least now we know.'

Jack's brother, who had travelled from Cornwall with his carer, arrived halfway through the day. He was eighty-two years old and the only words Kite heard him utter was that Jack had been a 'hard act to follow'. The constant stream of visitors gathered around the table eating, drinking and sharing memories. There was plenty of singing and storytelling at the Carrec Arms that afternoon, but Kite didn't hear much of it, because all that she could think of was her broken hearted great-grandmother, and how sad it was that she never got to tell her daughter, Kite's grandmother, that she was loved, and then there was Dawn, who had been so loved but had ended her life before it had started. None of it made any sense to her and what she was beginning to realize was how complicated life was, how full of challenges and secrets, even for these old people who she would have thought might have worked everything out by now.

Kite noticed that Seth disappeared a few times during the afternoon and when he came back he always smelt of smoke. The last time he popped out Dr Sherpa 'kept him company', and when they returned Seth began singing and strumming away at his guitar.

'You've got your Grandpa's voice, all right.' Aida started humming along, picking out lines of the story here and there in a surprisingly sweet and tuneful voice. The old men bickered with her over the lyrics.

'Don't go listening to these two. They never could hold a tune!' Aida laughed.

'Aye, well, that's as maybe, but we've been hard pushed hearing ourselves *think* all these years with you around, let alone *sing*!' Giles was smiling fondly at Aida. Until now Kite had never been much around so many old people, but despite all their arguments and bickering they seemed to know and accept each other as part of the landscape. She glanced over to the cap on Jack's empty chair; it seemed impossible that he wasn't somewhere nearby, tapping along to the music.

She wished that Lily could hear Seth's songs and that Hannah could have known her own story. And more than any of these things she wished that she could go back to London and walk down the stairs to Dawn's flat, sit on her bed and tell her all about this. She glanced outside to see that the light was fading. Tomorrow, she thought, if the wind is still raging I'll take my birthday kite and fly it for Dawn.

'You know I won't be able to stop here, don't you? I'm going to have to find the family of this Peter Klein,' Seth said as they drove back across the common. 'Who knows, maybe he's still alive.'

Kite nodded. She thought of old Jack's photos of his time in India . . . and about how Jack and Agnes had been secretly in love. It wasn't just where you were from; it was *all* the experiences that you drank in during your life that made you who you were. Despite everything, it was somehow comforting to know exactly how you stretched into the past and out across the world in all directions.

Skeletons

In the morning Kite walked over to the spyhole window and peered out. For the first time since they'd arrived she watched the glowering rainclouds brood over the mountain. To the left the woodland swayed in a wild wind dance.

Garth was waiting for her on the path below Mirror Falls. He wore sturdy new walking boots with a thick tread.

'Look for the bones under this ledge – that's what Gran said, isn't it?'

She nodded as Garth climbed on to the stone platform where the sheep carcass had lain. He held out his hand to help Kite down, but instead she slid along the rock and jumped the remaining distance herself. She felt as if she had been here before, in her dream. Garth eased himself over the ledge and found a foothold in the rock. The roar of the waterfall was at its most ferocious here. Garth ducked to see into the crevice and whistled as he realized how many bones lay there.

'I can see why Gran thought the owls were haunting her; they must have kept coming back looking for the barn and crashed to their deaths. You know they nest for generations in the same place. No wonder she couldn't live here with this on her conscience.'

Kite shivered. It was like discovering the aftermath of a massacre – and Agnes had hidden the evidence right here under her 'dream house'.

When they'd finally cleared out the crevice, the bones half filled both hessian sacks. They climbed in silence up the path and left them at the door.

Seth was sitting at the table eating breakfast.

'I'm helping Garth finish his sculpture,' announced Kite.

Seth looked up and tapped the newspaper – the *Cumbrian and Westmorland Herald*. 'I've been reading all about your commission from the National Trust!' He smiled at them both. 'Seems like Garth's garths are going to be all over the walkways of the Lakes! It says here your work is –' Seth put on what he called his 'proper posh' voice – '"A meditation on the erosion of time . . ."'

'Really! I didn't know that!' Garth laughed, then picked up the paper and read it for himself. 'Makes me sound good! I wish they'd told the Art GCSE markers though!'

'Why, what did you get?'

'A "D".'

Seth laughed and clapped him on the back.

'I'm just going up to pack a few things, in case it rains,' Kite called, running up the staircase. She placed the reed box in her backpack. It felt like time. She knew that Dawn wasn't angry with her and she also knew that she could never give her all the answers to her questions. What she could do was honour Dawn's memory and lay her spirit to rest in a beautiful place that Dawn would have loved, a place that Kite had come to love too. She picked up the feather and placed it back under her pillow. She had decided to keep it after all. The feather – and the birthday card, that she now turned over in her hands. I'll open it when I've buried the reed, she promised herself as she unhooked her tethered kite from the wall.

When they were gone, Seth wandered over to the large glass window and watched their journey through the valley. He saw Garth take Kite's hand and not let go. They disappeared from view as they descended the steep path that led down to the base of the waterfall.

Then further up the valley he saw a multicoloured kite begin to bob hopefully. The string seemed to get caught a couple of times before the kite lifted way off the ground and rose steadily, strongly, into the fading grey sky. So here at last were the moods of the mountains. Watching his daughter from this distance, Seth felt the tears stream down his cheeks.

When Garth and Kite reached the furthest part of the valley they stopped for a moment, turned and looked back towards Mirror Falls. Seth waved to Kite, though he knew that she would probably not be able to see him.

He looked up at the owl print on the glass. Only one wing was vaguely discernible now.

Cloudburst

A herd of sheep gathered off the fell and huddled together, forming an orderly line in the shelter of a drystone wall.

'They always know when it's going to be really bad,' Garth told her as they packed away the kite.

Sure enough, it wasn't long before the thick black clouds that swirled across the top of the mountains gathered speed . . . and then came the cloudburst. Kite opened her mouth and drank. Her cheeks stung with the constant pressure of the sharp rain, but she was glad that there was nowhere to shelter. She felt alive in every cell of her body for the first time in ages as they began to climb the steep path over Kite Carrec. Kite peered up at the grey mountain that had been so green and sunny on their last walk together. Holding on to each other, they slipped here and there in the stream that was already beginning to cascade down the track.

By the time they'd descended the slope into the

reservoir they were both soaked and mud-smeared. The rain had taken only a few minutes to penetrate Kite's thin cagoule. Garth handed her his padded jacket, his damp shirt clinging close to his body.

Together they placed all the owl bones deep into the sheep's belly and sealed them in with slates. As Garth worked he seemed to forget that the rain was falling.

'Do you think you can find a place for this?'

Kite took the little box from her pocket. She lifted out the reed and handed it to Garth. He turned it over in his hands with great care, just as he had in her dream.

'Dawn's golden reed,' she whispered.

Garth lodged it firmly among the slates, stones and bones of his sculpture. When the reservoir filled and the sheep was underwater, maybe all these tiny shards of history would float away from the sculpture: the trout that Seth had caught for Jack, Agnes's owl bones and Dawn's music. They were all now part of the story of this place.

'Do you want to sit and watch it disappear?' asked Garth.

Kite nodded through chattering teeth and Garth grabbed her hand and started to run with her across the bridge and up a steep rocky slope. They were high above the dam now and Kite turned to look down to where the boundary walls and the little bridge were already beginning to be submerged.

'Come and watch it from here!'

A thick overhang of rock served as a secure roof sloping low on both sides so that the water drained off the edges, leaving the view over the dam clear.

Garth rummaged in the back of the cave and found a hessian sack full of dry twigs and wood.

'This is my place where I like to come, to be alone with all this!' Garth spread out his arms, taking in the lake and surrounding mountains with his gesture. He stacked the twigs into a pile and took out a lighter. The fire was slow to start and smoked for a while, but Garth kept piling twigs on until bright orange flames started to rise up.

'Thank you!' Kite said as she warmed her hands.

'What for?'

'Bringing me here, listening to me, helping me through.'

She laid her head on his shoulder and they watched the rain pour over the ledge and steam mingle with smoke from the fire. She felt his fingers lift a strand of her hair and twist it around and around, making perfect spirals. He bent down slowly and kissed the top of her head and she could feel what was coming next. She pulled away from him.

'I can't,' she said with a sigh. 'I feel as if I've just buried my friend.'

Garth nodded and placed an arm around her shoulder, pulling her close to him. She could feel his heart beating against her chest and she closed her eyes. She listened to the rain falling and the crackling of the fire and then she heard another sound, warm and free and golden. Dawn's music rose up from where the reed lay lodged between slates and bones, up into the air and travelled through the valley towards her, coursing along her blood stream, up through her spine and into her heart.

At first it came upon her gently like a whisper of sadness blowing through her, but then the tears were rolling freely down her face and her chest ached, as if her ribcage was about to crack open with surging grief. Now her breath came in great sobs that she had no control over. She felt Garth draw her closer to him, but he didn't speak or try to quiet the emotion in her. The rain poured over the edge of the rock and the reservoir below began to fill with water. The tears that she had held back for so long, tears for the friend she would never see again, fell hard and strong, building in force, not weakening, as she let them flow.

Birthday Card

It was not until morning that Kite realized that the owl print was gone.

'As if it had never been . . .' she whispered.

'Well, I just hope we make it through this weather!' Seth muttered to Dr Sherpa, Ellie and the rest of the little group that had gathered outside the Carrec Arms. Just as they were about to leave Aida wheeled herself up to the car and gave Seth a hand-sewn leather deer.

'This is the toy that Peter, your grandad, made!'

'Thank you, Aida!' Seth clasped it in his hands delightedly.

The car started on the third attempt. The little windscreen wipers swished back and forth, desperately trying to keep up with the constant rivulets of rain pooling against the bonnet. As they drove slowly along, the girl with pink hair came running out of a little stone cottage. Not seeming to mind about the rain, she stood and waved.

'Who's that?' asked Seth.

'Cassie.' Kite waved back.

'Seems like you've made some friends around here.'

Kite smiled. She looked down at the little slate necklace Garth had given her and thought how much she would miss these people and this place.

The windows were steaming up. Since she was little Kite had always loved the feeling of lying across the back seat of the car driving through the rain, all cosy and safe whatever was happening outside. Seth's shoulders were hunched in concentration as he kept slowing to clear the mist on the inside of the windscreen.

Kite placed her hand in her pocket and slipped out Dawn's card, opened it and read the words that she knew could not be avoided any longer.

Dear Kite,
Happy Birthday my best friend, my 'thithter'!
Love Dawn
XXX

A small sharp noise escaped from her mouth. Just as Hazel had said, there was no explanation here, nothing. Slowly she closed the card and turned it over to see the image on the front and, as she did, she had to struggle to catch her breath. In her hands she held a photograph of a great white owl soaring over a mountain range, her wings lit up against a starry night sky.

Part Three
Returning

Epilogue

The Hardest Things

Kite had seen Lucy the counsellor as soon as she'd got back, on Dr Sherpa's suggestion. She'd felt ready to speak of everything she had felt, everything she was still feeling, and it was reassuring to know that whenever she needed her Lucy was there. But the person who helped her the most over the next two years was Miss Choulty.

Kite had missed her in school while she'd been on maternity leave and had spontaneously hugged her when she'd called round to check that Kite was 'getting through'. It felt strange to be sitting with Miss Choulty, talking of Dawn, as she fed her newborn baby, and yet somehow comforting to witness what Miss Choulty called her 'miracle of happiness' that she had named 'Hope'.

'What are the hardest things to cope with?' Miss Choulty asked as she placed Hope in Kite's arms.

There had been so many hardest things . . .

Coming back to Fairview to find that a young

couple had moved into Dawn's flat. Jess's cat flap had been boarded up and the door painted a creamy yellow colour. Instead of Dawn's music through the wall she'd heard their baby crying, laughing and gurgling. Over the next two years, as she took her GCSEs and finished her first year of A levels, she had watched little Ebony grow. The day when Jodie and Richard had asked her to babysit she'd had palpitations, wondering whether she would actually be able to step foot inside Dawn's bedroom. What do you expect to find? she reasoned with herself. Dawn has gone. Nothing of her is here any more. As soon as she entered the flat she knew that that was true. Like Ruby, Jodie was a fan of colour and every room had been repainted. The living room was a rich, cosy orange and Ebony's bedroom was painted in shocking pink, a far cry from the delicate duck-egg blue it had once been. As Kite peered into Dawn's bedroom from the doorway Jodie came to stand by her side.

'It's OK, Kite; we know what happened to your friend. I'm so sorry!'

A feeling of relief washed over Kite. The only ghosts of Dawn that lived in the flat were the ghosts of her own memories. Sometimes she let them play over her and sometimes she knew that if she was to carry on and do her A levels and babysit for Ebony, if she was to live and grow, she could not let visions of Dawn, either in her waking moments or her sleep, take her over as they had once done.

It had taken her weeks to pluck up the courage to call Hazel and Jimmy at their new home. That had been one of the hardest 'hardest things'. Jimmy answered the phone and there had been a long pause after she'd said, 'Hi, it's Kite,' because for years, her next line had always been, 'Is Dawn there, please?' But they had not talked about Dawn. 'Remember that job I was going for?' Jimmy asked Kite. She had forgotten, but she did remember now that he'd worn the interview suit at Dawn's funeral. 'Well, I got it. Anyway, don't know why I thought of that really, but Hazel and I don't work shifts now; it makes life a bit easier. I'll ask Hazel to call you, though it's hard, you know. Don't be offended if she can't bring herself to.'

For the first few days afterwards Kite had listened out for the phone, but the call from Hazel never came.

At school everyone was kind and sensitive towards her and went out of their way to draw her into their friendship folds. But she couldn't always bring herself to be with them in the places that she would have hung out with Dawn. Of course she had the excuse of having to catch up and actually take her GCSEs before she could start on her A-level courses with the others, and that provided her with the get-out she sometimes needed.

It had been Garth's suggestion that she go to a concert, when she'd told him how much she missed the sound of Dawn's playing through her bedroom wall. One day she contacted Esme and Eddie on

Facebook and that's how she found herself in a concert hall, listening to them play.

Some of the hardest moments of all were when she felt happy. On her third week back Jacey and Laura from running club had turned up at her front door. They were training for a team run and they *needed* her, they said. It took her two months to get back to fitness, but she found that the running took her out of her head. Sometimes they would chat as they ran along, talking about nonsensical things that happened at school, a film someone had seen, an outrageous post on Facebook, who fancied who, and she would run along and just listen. After a few weeks she would find herself laughing at something, and feel only a wisp of sadness that she had not been able to share the joke with Dawn.

The race they'd entered was a county championship. As Seth and Ruby drove her on to the car park of the muddy field she suddenly lost her nerve. She had almost dropped out, but it was a recollection of Dawn at her last race that made her carry on.

As she lay collapsed in a great heap of wet clay at the finish line, Dawn stared down at Kite and giggled her infectious little giggle.

'You did it! You beat your best time!' she shouted, throwing Kite a towel.

Something had changed in the way memories of Dawn came back to her. She was no longer dissecting every conversation they'd ever had, searching for reasons why. Now her memories were often of the happy, random times they'd spent together, and when she was transported back to them she would, more often than not, feel bolstered and encouraged, rather than burdened.

'Thank you, Dawn,' she said as her spikes ploughed up the thick clay, her heart pumping hard. She could feel her lungs opening as she pounded the ground and began to pass other coloured bibs. When she faced the last hill she thought of Jack running up Kite Carrec and her legs extended further. At the top Ruby and Seth were jumping up and down in a frenzy of excitement calling her name.

'Run, Kite, run!' Before she knew what was happening she was being funnelled into the finishing lane. Seth ran over, lifted her up and twirled her around, mud flying in every direction. The feeling Kite had at that moment was one of pure joy, and she was relieved that she could still feel it, even though the fact remained that happy moments in a world without Dawn were also the hardest things to bear. They had always turned up to support each other on big occasions. More and more she called on these happy memories of Dawn so that she could carry her best friend with her through all the important days of her life.

It had taken a lot longer to try to fly again. One day she'd overheard Ruby talking on the phone: 'You won't stop calling, will you? I'm sure she'll come back in time, so please keep trying.'

Annalisa had more than lived up to her promise, calling regularly until finally she'd come and knocked at their door. At first Kite hardly recognized her with her new shock of bright red hair cut into a sleek bob and finished off with a sequinned bandanna.

'I *adore* the flowers!' Annalisa enthused, looking down at the sculptural orange heads of the birds of paradise. 'It is not possible to have these exquisite birds outside your door and never fly!'

Annalisa sat in her cross-legged yoga position on Kite's bed. 'I know you have your examinations to catch up on, but Ruby says you are doing well and must have a break from revision.'

Kite lowered her eyes.

It was difficult to describe even to herself what had stopped her from going back to Circus Space, except that it would feel like she was moving on and fulfilling her dreams without her best friend.

'I know this doesn't make any sense, but I feel like it's a sort of betrayal.'

'So remind me . . . what was the last message of your friend?'

Kite stood on her bed and took down the birthday card, with the Dawn owl feather inside. 'I think it was probably this.'

Annalisa ran her fingers over the feather, examined the image on the front of the card, and raised her eyebrows. 'Exactly,' she seemed to say.

Kite stood and looked at herself in the mirror. She was taller and stronger, and after all her training at Circus Space over the past six months she had finally lost her skinny-little-girl straight-up-and-down figure. People who hadn't seen her for a while commented on how much she'd 'matured'. Mali has whistled when he'd first seen her and asked her out again almost straight away. She'd told him that she liked him 'much better as a friend'. 'That's the line no one wants to hear!' he'd joked. Then what was it that Grandma Grace had said when she came to visit last month . . . ?

'You've bloomed, my darlin'.'

But if she had changed on the outside, the real growing she had done was invisible to most people around her. It had taken time to understand that she would never be the old Kite again, that what Dawn had done had changed her forever.

Kite cried most of the morning on what would have been Dawn's eighteenth birthday, but she'd eventually got herself dressed and was heading out to Circus Space when there was a knock at the door.

She opened it and there was Hazel, who had also been crying. She was holding a photograph album in her hands, which she offered up to Kite.

'I was trying to work out who would understand how I feel today,' she wept.

They sat and looked through the photographs of Kite and Dawn from the ages of five to sixteen. Here was a record of all that had been good and happy and funny and plain stupid about all the things that they had done together. Hazel and Kite had laughed and cried and when the album was closed and neither of them had any tears left Hazel got up to leave.

'I'm on my way to Circus Space; I was wondering if you'd like to come with me,' Kite asked tentatively.

Hazel reached out for Kite's hand and nodded. 'I'll never forget how you came to sit by my side at Dawn's funeral,' she whispered, squeezing Kite's hand firmly in her own.

Kite had got to know Garth much better since she left the Lakes. He'd visited her in London for a few days before leaving for New Zealand and they'd trailed around galleries, talking and finding out the kind of things they'd never asked each other before. She knew now what music he liked, how much he'd enjoyed his work in the outward-bound centre, that he planned to go to art college in Manchester but that he felt 'like a fish out of water' in the city. Since he'd been in New Zealand they'd phoned and emailed and he, who had claimed to be backward with technology, had even got into Skype and Facebook and now they posted photos and messages to each other every day.

Kite picked up the little collection of hand-made postcards that he'd sent her over the last two years. Some of them were sketches of the abstract-looking sculptures he'd built in the sheepfolds for his commission. Kite had talked so much about Garth to Esme recently that she'd asked if they were going out. Kite laughed at the thought of it because you could hardly call someone trying to kiss you once over two years ago and a collection of postcards (no matter how much thought had gone into the drawing of them) 'going out'. She shuffled the cards in her hands and turned the most recent one over and read it for the hundredth time. Maybe it was because the distance was so great between them that she missed him so much now. It felt like an age till Christmas.

Dear Kite,

I never thought I would think anywhere as beautiful as the Lakes. This is a sketch of me and my dad sitting by Lake Taupo (largest lake in New Zealand). It puts me in mind of Kite Carrec. Thinking maybe you might want to visit me when I get back . . . how does Christmas in the Lakes sound?

Can't wait to see you,

Love,

Garth

She didn't really know what they would mean to each other now or how she would feel about him when she returned to the Lake District. But she knew what he'd been to her and she would never forget the way that he'd held her when she'd been the closest she had ever felt to falling.

Now here she was on the train staring out of the window and watching the frozen landscape changing. A single tree in the middle of an icy field reminded Kite of how she had felt inside when she last travelled up to the Lake District. She felt relieved that the weather and the season could not have been more different than on her previous visit. In places it was difficult to tell where the land ended and the sky began as the powder snow began to cover houses, buildings and trees and seemed to smooth out all the hard edges of the world. Smoke rose from farm and cottage chimneys and Kite thought of the welcoming amber glow of the Carrec Arms and Ellie lighting the fire for Jack.

She contemplated the snow as it covered every imperfection in the landscape.

'I love it when it snows,' Dawn said as they waited at the bottom of the steps for Jimmy to take them sledging. 'It makes everything look so perfect. I never want to spoil it by treading in it.'

'I can never wait to jump in!' Kite laughed, grabbing a great handful of snow and lobbing it at Dawn.

On their way home Jimmy let the snow settle in the palm of his hand. 'Do you know, every single flake is different? If you look at these under a microscope no two are the same.' Dawn peered up at Jimmy, her serious little face full of wonder.

'Like you two – chalk and cheese!' He laughed as he tugged them along on the sledge.

Kite smiled. She had come to love the flow of memories that played through her like music.

She felt in her pocket for Dawn's reed box that she always carried with her. It was comforting to hold it close.

Kite sat in the plush velvet seats of the auditorium waiting for the musicians to enter. People were gathering all around her, sorting out their coats and looking through programmes. She glanced down at the one Dawn had given her and searched out her friend's name. She felt ridiculously proud. The musicians entered the stage in their sections. The wind instruments sat together on a platform above the violins. Dawn blushed bright red as she settled herself in her seat and then stood and played the top A that the whole orchestra tuned up to.

Kite watched the conductor in his long black coat as Dawn played, his hands instructing her to come in lightly and smoothly. Just before she began her first solo Kite held her breath. She could read the tension in Dawn's face and watched as she made tiny adjustments and readjustments to the reed.

Now Kite felt the tension in her own body until the first note of Dawn's solo emerged rich and clear. Then she began to enjoy it, as Dawn too relaxed into the music. She felt her heart leap and her emotions soar. As she watched, Kite understood that Dawn's playing was her way of flying.

There was applause all round and people were giving the orchestra a standing ovation.

The lady next to her handed her a tissue. 'Brahms can do that to you,' she said with a smile, and Kite realized that she had been crying with pride.

Now the conductor was asking Dawn to stand up. She looked mortified but he insisted and the audience kept on clapping too, demanding her to take a special bow.

'Why has he picked her out?' Kite asked the woman as she thanked her for the tissues and wiped her eyes.

'Because that girl is going to be great.'

Kite wiped the tears from her eyes and reached up for Grandma Grace's St Christopher. 'You keep wearing it, my sweetheart,' was the last thing Grace had said to her before going back to St Kitts. Kite rummaged in her bag and took out Garth's slate necklace. She hung it round her neck, pulling the leather fastening tighter. It was the first time she had worn it. Then she plugged in her iPod and listened to the end of Seth's new album. It had taken him over two years to write but it had re-launched his career. He was often away now, playing concerts and festivals. Finding out about his family seemed to have given Seth so much more than just this album, Kite thought, as she listened to the confident, sombre music on *The Song of Storeys*. This last track he had called 'For Dawn'.

Kite looked in her hand mirror and wiped her eyes. 'The road should be long and winding.' Tears came easily to her these days, but Lucy had told her that it was a good sign and so she never tried to stop them. She ruffled up her hair, so long now that it cascaded down her back to the base of her spine, then took out the brown eyeliner she'd bought at Euston station and underlined her eyes as Dawn had once taught her to do. She turned to the side to see the tiny sea-green jewel that glinted in her nose, her eighteenth birthday present from Ruby and Seth. She smoothed her short velvet paisley-print skirt over her thick leggings and retied the ribbons on her new cherry DMs.

Garth was standing on the snowy station waiting for her. Bardsey sat faithfully beside him. It was comical how their heads scanned the platform in the same direction, searching for her. Garth was wearing a serious-looking padded parker. He looked taller and broader in the shoulders and back, but maybe it was down to the layers he was wearing against the cold. Kite threw on the oversized sheepskin jacket that Seth had allowed her to pinch off him. As soon as she stepped off the train she was greeted by a loud bark and Bardsey bounded towards her, leaping at her as if he'd been longing for her to come back. Kite laughed and brushed the snow from her clothes.

'You should have seen the greeting I got when I came back from New Zealand!' Garth walked towards her with his long arms flung open wide, like the Angel of the North. Kite smiled inwardly at the thought. It was what she'd found different about him when they'd first met, and what she'd grown to like about him. It didn't seem to occur to him to hide how he felt. They stood and held each other without speaking, their combined breaths visible in the cold bright air. Her heart thudded in her chest as she hugged this boy who seemed to understand her better than anyone. She pulled away from him in case he felt the intensity of her feelings towards him. What if he didn't feel the same way? But as they parted he let his hand rest on the back of her head as if he didn't want to let her go.

'You're wearing my slate-stone.' Garth touched the leather pendant, grazing the skin on her neck as he did so. She nodded, feeling the heat rise to her cheeks.

'So how was it? Seeing your dad?' she asked.

Garth furrowed his forehead. 'We had a fair bit of talking to do, but we had some good times together. He's coming back to visit next year, so we'll see.'

'You can sit together on that carved seat you made for him.' Kite smiled. 'Remember the deer?'

'I remember the sun on your hair . . .' he let his fingers trace the length of it down her back.

'Isn't this Dr Sherpa's old Land Rover?' Kite asked, taking a deep, calming breath as she climbed in.

'Not any more. He sold it to Gran.'

Kite could not imagine the Agnes Landseer she had known driving around in this. She was glad that she had not come back in summer, glad that everything looked so different with the ground frozen and the sky heavy with snow, and all this made her feel as if the world was new and peaceful and settled . . . until they began to drive up the now smooth path that lead to Mirror Falls. Halfway up was a new sign: 'Mirror Falls Visitor Centre'.

'Gran's set up a sort of sanctuary for nature lovers,' Garth explained.

That slow climb up the track stirred up all the old emotions and she found herself gently weeping. Garth took one hand off the steering wheel and reached for hers.

Kite took a deep breath as they stepped through the familiar glass entrance to be greeted by a cheerful woman with a sleek silver bob and a flash of crimson lipstick. She walked around the reception desk and offered Kite the warmest of hugs. If she had seen her on a street in London she would have walked straight past her, she bore so little resemblance to the Agnes Landseer she'd known only two years before. If only Dawn had understood this, as Agnes had, as she herself had – that you could come back from feeling low, that things could always change, unless you stopped life in its tracks.

Bardsey led the way and the three of them took the path down by the waterfall and past the stone ledge. Kite's mind spiralled down too: now she was staring through the stepping stones at a sheep carcass, now she crouched next to the Dawn owl, now she was feeling the power of water rushing over stone as Garth handed her bone after bone to place in the hessian sack. She had come, with the help of Lucy and Miss Choulty, to understand all the strange happenings and sightings of Dawn at Mirror Falls as a reflection of her own mind after Dawn committed suicide, but now that she was here it all seemed so real again.

They walked beyond the waterfall, trudging through untrodden snow to the base of the chasm, following the line of the stream far enough to turn and look up at what had once been the large sheet-glass window view on to the valley, the same window that the imprint of the Dawn owl had clung on to for so long. Apart from a slit of open glass through which a few birdwatchers' telescopes protruded, the whole of the front of the building had been clad in slate.

'Not as perfect as it was, but at least we've had no more owls crashing in on us,' Agnes explained. 'I'll let you tell.' She patted Garth on the shoulder and winked at him playfully. 'Leave Bardsey here with me – you two have a lot of catching up to do.'

'Tell me what?' Kite asked as they climbed back into the Land Rover.

Garth smiled his wide warm smile but didn't answer. They headed out to the Haweswater Dam in silence.

'What do you want to do now?' Garth asked as he pulled into the car park. It felt to Kite as if the Land Rover was about to combust with the force of the charged energy between them.

'Let's run!' Kite leaped from the car with Garth close on her heels. Together they ploughed up the snow that scrunched satisfyingly beneath their feet.

'You're on!'

As they ran up the fell the snow began to fall, lightly at first and then heavier. The last time she'd run up here she'd been pitifully weak. Now her body felt strong and fit and able to carry her up even the steepest of fells in the deepening snow.

'You can run!' Garth laughed as she kept pace with him over the final stretch of ground that led to the cave. They lay on the cold rock until they got their breath back. Kite turned her head to Garth so that their breath mist mingled together.

'I always could run . . . before . . .' Kite faltered.

He sensed her change of mood and sat up a little way apart from her.

She pulled her body upright too and they surveyed the lake as the snow landed and melted on its surface.

It seemed like a dream now that they had really stood in the dry reservoir together building the sheep sculpture and burying Dawn's reed. Now everything was submerged deep, deep underwater. Kite surveyed the smooth white landscape that made everything look perfect for a while. But what she had come to accept was that under the surface of everything was the constant presence of Dawn, what Dawn had been and what Dawn had done and what Dawn would have been doing now if she was still alive.

'I'd like to go to Old Jack's grave, buy you a drink in the Carrec Arms and see Ellie and Cassie and Dr Sherpa to say thank you for all they did for me . . . and Seth's sent a photo of Peter's sister in Germany for me to give to Aida . . .' Kite told Garth.

'Aida died just a few weeks ago. Did you not hear?'

Kite shook her head. She felt strangely sad that she couldn't tell Aida the end of the story about Lily, her best friend. How Kite and Seth had made the trip together to the nursing home in Hamburg and Kite had been moved by the whole experience. It was a sweet photo that she now showed Garth of her great-grandfather's sister Anna holding the little leather deer made by her brother Peter, which Aida had given to Seth.

'She had a collection of her own just like the one Aida gave us.'

'Poor Aida!' Garth sighed. 'She would have liked

to hear of that. But maybe she's somewhere out there listening!'

It was something that Kite had thought about a lot over the past two years. What happens after you die? The only conclusion she could come to was that somewhere inside her she would always carry something of Dawn's spirit.

Garth turned towards her and stared straight into her eyes. There was a light playfulness glinting in his gaze that she didn't remember seeing there before.

'You know, you stared at me like this on the first day I met you . . . If it was because you thought I looked like a foreigner, you were wrong! It turns out I'm just as much a part of this place as you!' Kite said, shaking her head forward and throwing it back again to shift the powder snow that had settled on her hair.

Garth looked down at his hands and shook his head. 'It wasn't that . . . I'm no good at words. I was actually staring because I wanted to paint you.'

'Those are quite good words!' Kite laughed as she brushed the snow off Garth's coat, but he didn't reach out to her. Maybe, after last time, he was waiting for her to make the first move. She leaned slowly towards him and kissed him gently on the lips. The freezing cold tips of their noses touched, and they pulled apart, laughing. Then he lifted her chin up towards him so that they were staring into each other's eyes again. He traced his fingers over her scar-brow and around her face, pausing on the little nose jewel and tracing her jaw around to the nape of her neck, where he gathered a thick clump of her hair into his hands. He leaned down and kissed her eyelids. She felt his arm curl under her coat and around her waist as she cleaved towards him and their lips met again with a passion and longing that took her breath away.

Eventually they drew apart and he wrapped his arm around her shoulders. She let her head rest against him.

'Can I?'

'Can you what?'

'Draw you, right here?' Garth asked, rummaging in his pocket for a sketchbook and charcoal pencil.

'You planned this!' Kite joked, sitting up.

'I've had long enough. Anyway, I'll not get to art college without drawing what inspires me.' Garth smiled at her, picked up his pencil and began his portrait.

Kite felt Garth's intense gaze on her as she took in the beauty and quiet of the place. Every sense in her body felt cushioned and protected. The early-evening light was silvery white and she watched as the snowflakes fell and melted on the lake.

Kite half expected to hear Dawn's music playing through the perfect acoustic of the snowy valley, but there was nothing but a deep and sombre silence.

*

It was dusk when they approached Scar View. Garth pulled up on the road and turned off the headlights.

'Wrap up, put your gloves on,' he ordered, grabbing a silly red bobble hat and scrunching it on Kite's head. Then he climbed a stile, holding out his hand for Kite.

'There was a bonny lass sat upon a stile!' he sang.

'You've got a terrible voice!' Kite laughed, jumping down and picking up a great handful of snow, patting it in her hands and lobbing it at him!

'Thanks!'

Kite began to run through the snowy field as Garth pursued her. His snowball caught the back of her head and she collapsed laughing. Garth lay next to her as she stretched out her arms and legs to form the shape of a snow angel.

Garth stretched out his own arms so that their fingertips on one hand touched.

'What are we doing here?' Kite giggled.

'You'll see!'

As she felt her breathing settle back to normal Kite stared up at the faint outline of a crescent moon.

Garth placed his fingers to his lips and then pointed upward. Kite's heart leaped out of her as she followed the path of a pair of owls soaring side by side through the silver-grey sky.

Acknowledgements

Thanks go to my husband Leo and children Maya, Keshin and Esha-Lily for their support in the writing of this book, and a special thanks to my son Keshin Harrison, whose soulful composing, singing and songwriting has inspired the character of Seth.

Thank you to my lovely agent Sophie Gorell Barnes of MBA Literary Agents for her constant support and insight into the writing process.

I would like to thank my talented and insightful editors Sam Swinnerton, Ruth Alltimes and Emma Young for guiding me through the journey of writing this book.

Readers often ask me about all the different people who help to bring a book to publication. The following people at Macmillan Children's Books have all played an important part in helping me to capture the 'Kite Spirit' of this book: Belinda Rasmussen (Publisher), Polly Nolan (Associate Publishing Director), Catherine Alport (Publicity Manager), Louise McKee (Marketing Manager), Rachel Vale (Art Director), Tracey Ridgewell (Senior Text Designer), Fliss Stevens (Managing Editor), Talya Baker (Copy-editor) and Wendy Plovmand (Illustrator). Thank you, all.

My sincere and heartfelt thanks go to my friend Astrid Griffiths for sharing her own experience and enabling me to fully understand the emotional depths of shock, trauma and the long and painful legacy of grief that suicide causes. It was important for us both to treat the subject with respect, truthfulness and sensitivity, and in all of this Astrid has been my guide.

I am indebted to my friend Ruth Bolister, who has taught me more about the craft of making reeds and what goes into playing the oboe than anyone would normally have access to. Her exquisite playing meanders through the pages of *Kite Spirit*.

To my mum Freda Brahmachari, who shared with me stories of her own childhood growing up in Cumbria. To my aunty Marylynne Winder, who walked the fells with me and told me tales of digging beneath rock and bone and feeling the spirits of the landscape.

To the degree students at the Circus Space in London, who inspired me to create the character of Kite.

With thanks for medical advice from my friend Dr Beth Macmillan.

References

References to local history and traditions such as that of the 'Passing Bell' I have drawn from the book *Ploughing in Latin: A History of Bampton*, ed. Jane Gregg, Bookcase 2003.

Background to fell running was garnered from *Feet in the Clouds: A Story of Fell Running and Obsession* by Richard Askwith and Robert Macfarlane, Aurum Press Ltd 2005.

The seed of the idea for 'Mirror Falls' came from watching The Balancing Barn in Suffolk being built, and the wonderful series of contemporary buildings that are part of Living Architecture. 'Mirror Falls', however, can only be visited in the imagination!

The Romantic poet William Wordsworth's 'The Prelude' and the artist-sculptors Andy Goldsworthy, Antony Gormley and Richard Long were all inspirations in the writing of this book.

Advice and support

Here is a list of organizations and websites where you will find confidential support if you need advice and don't feel that you can turn to a member of your family, a friend, a teacher, a school counsellor or a GP.

YoungMinds

YoungMinds is a national charity committed to improving the mental health and emotional well-being of children and young people. All calls from the UK are free. If you are a young person experiencing a mental health crisis, text YM to 85258 for free 24/7 support across the UK.

Parents Helpline : 0808 802 5544

Website : www.youngminds.org.uk

Mind

Mind is a mental-health charity covering both England and Wales. The Mind InfoLine offers confidential help on a range of mental-health issues.

Call 0300 123 3393 or text 86463 for information and support.

Website : www.mind.org.uk

The Samaritans

If you're experiencing depression, the Samaritans provide confidential non-judgemental emotional support. Lines are open 24 hours a day, 365 days a year. Calls are free from any phone.

Tel : 116123

Website : www.samaritans.org

ChildLine

If you are worried about anything – it could be something big or something small – don't bottle it up. It can really help if you talk to someone. If there is something on your mind, ChildLine is here for you for free confidential support.

Tel : 0800 1111

Website : www.childline.org.uk

The Holding Collective

This is a social enterprise supporting children and families with their emotional wellbeing.

Website : www.theholdingcollective.com

Papyrus

This is the UK Charity for the prevention of young suicide. Their service, HopelineUK is a specialist telephone service staffed by trained professionals who give non-judgemental support, practical advice and information to children, teenagers and young people up to the age of 35 who are worried about how they are feeling or anyone who is concerned about a young person. Whatever you are going through, call free anytime.

Tel: 0800 068 4141 or 077866209697

Website : www.papyrus-uk.org